Born in Romania, Mihaela fir[illegible] journalist whilst studying history and po[illegible]niversity of Iasi. In 2016, she came to the United Kingdom as a diplomat and after finishing her five-year mandate, decided to remain in London and make it her second home.

She loves to read mystery books and passionately listens to the life stories of the people that she meets during her activities. She believes that life is full of interesting characters and hidden stories. You just have to lend an ear and understand…

To my dear parents, Angela and Constantin Enache

Mihaela Enache

THE SAD STORY OF DIANE DUNMORE

AUSTIN MACAULEY PUBLISHERS™
LONDON • CAMBRIDGE • NEW YORK • SHARJAH

This is a work of fiction. Names, characters, businesses, places, events, locales, and incidents are either the products of the author's imagination or used in a fictitious manner. Any resemblance to actual persons, living or dead, or actual events is purely coincidental.

A CIP catalogue record for this title is available from the British Library.

ISBN 9781035863068 (Paperback)
ISBN 9781035863075 (ePub e-book)

www.austinmacauley.com

First Published 2024
Austin Macauley Publishers Ltd®
1 Canada Square
Canary Wharf
London
E14 5AA

A Morbid Discovery in the Library

Kristin had woken up this morning with a deep sense of anxiety and the feeling that she was going to have an unusual day at work. Maybe because she had had an unpleasant conversation with Chris the night before. She had tried, again without much success, to persuade him to move in together, to start a new life as a couple. She was fed up with the uncertainty of his presence at dinner and the hasty departures to the house where he lived with his wife, Diane. Kristin approached the prison library and distractedly fumbled for one of the three keys in the little pouch on her belt with which she then opened the massive wooden door and iron grill. She entered the library and noticed with a sense of relief, as usual, the presence of her boss, Eleonor Wilson, working behind the computer. Kristin was not afraid to work on her own with the residents, but she preferred to know Eleonor was there in the event of a crisis or a binding decision.

"Good morning, Eleonor," she said briskly.

"Morning, Kristin, I hope you are better today," answered Eleonor, looking at her over the top of her glasses.

"Yes, a little better. I'm getting used to autumn and these shorter days. I really do not like November. Who likes them actually?" She answered and sat down in one of the chairs next to Eleonor's desk.

"Well, some people adapt better to autumn time," said Eleonor, "others find it more difficult. How was yesterday in the afternoon, all good in here?"

"Oh, yes, our regular readers," Kristin said. "Helen was very helpful with the loan processing. In addition, she managed to find the DVDs for the *Originals* series, remember I couldn't find them. They were mixed in with the DVDs returned last week, I had forgotten to process them. And Grace didn't come in the afternoon, she said she was at the gym."

"Yes, Grace told me she wouldn't come in the afternoon. But she was very efficient yesterday morning. And yes, I agree with you, Helen is a very organised girl, I will give her positive references."

Kristin nodded absently as she hung up her jacket and got ready for work. Grace and Helen were orderlies, prisoners 'employed' in the library. They had been selected to work in the library a few months ago after an interview with Eleonor. Most of the female prisoners were applying for a different job in Clayton Prison departments, it was quite a tight competition. Some were working in the kitchen, garden, administrative or medical services as orderlies. They took symbolic salaries and tried to have a life like those outside. Some residents consider work as good therapy.

Eleonor was scanning the barcodes of the books, and the DVDs returned the day before. She looked a little concerned, and Kristin was sure that she was thinking of her older daughter who was suffering from a chronic depression caused by a failed relationship over a year ago.

"I hope Ellie is better," Kristin said, trying to put a certain compassion into her voice. She hadn't met the girl so far, but she really felt for her after that unhappy love story.

"Yes, she is, I think. She started a yoga session, and I am trying to encourage her, I do hope it helps. You know, Eleonor," said changing the topic, "they called us earlier from the gate entrance. We got two large boxes of newspapers; I suspect they are the last issue of *News Inside Prison*. Would you be so kind and get the boxes here, please? You know that it is very popular, the girls asked me yesterday when the November issue comes out. Then, I must admit, I am curious if Grace's poem has been published. I sent it a long time ago." She smiled absently, thinking of Grace's seraphic face.

"Sure, I'm going right now, I'll take the trolley first," Kristin said. *News Inside Prison* was an interesting newspaper with lots of information about life in prisons in England. They published poems and articles written by prisoners but also useful information for prison employees, available jobs or open debates on wages or work in prison-related topics.

Kristin hurried to the *Harper Room*, one of the library work rooms, to retrieve the trolley from the small storage room, hoping that Eleonor had sorted out the problem of one of its four wheels that got on her nerves during the last few weeks. She unlocked the storage room door and looked around for the trolley. Then, she saw the little corpse crouched in a corner of the storage room, looking like a little miserable marionette. She leaned slowly against the edge of the door like in a dream with her gaze fixed on the corpse. It was Diane, and Kristin *knew* she was dead. A trickle of blood had flowed from the top of her head and was visible on her forehead. The eyes were fixed on the floor with an ironic and contemptuous expression. *Good heavens*, thought Kristin, *even dead Diane keeps this contemptuous attitude*.

Kristin mechanically turned and left the room.

"Isn't it there?" She heard Eleonor's voice as if in a dream.

"I think it's Diane there," she said, "dead…"

"What are you talking about, where?" Eleonor whispered imperceptibly and ran to the *Harper Room*.

There was a moment of silence and Kristin hoped that Eleonor would not lose her temper, then she heard her saying in a trembling voice, "We must call the security service, they will call the local police, ugh, poor girl, what a nightmare…"

Kristin rose quietly from her chair and searched for the little leaflet phone book. Eleonor was already holding it with trembling hands, frantically searching for the phone numbers.

"Let's talk to Mary first, we must stick to the protocol. Go to her office and tell her to come here, please. Her phone is busy now. I'm going to call the security service in the meantime," Eleonor added.

Mary Thomson was the manager of the education department, their coordinator. She had her office in the same building, next door. Pale and silent, Kristin fumbled for the key, unlocked the door, and strode down the long corridor to the education department.

One Hour Later...

An investigation team from *Bradford West Police* sealed off the two access doors to Clayton Prison's library and began to work. Eleonor Wilson and Kristin Burton were in a room in the education department with Mary Thompson. Still in shock, they were waiting to talk to police officers.

Detectives Carol Thomas and Gareth Donovan were on their regular patrol route when received the call from BWP headquarters to proceed to Clayton Prison to begin an investigation into a suspicious death in the prison library. On their way, the two detectives tried to find out further information about the prison.

"Category C prison," Gareth Donovan said, reading from his mobile phone, "about 215 residents, women transgender, most with sentences between two and 20 years and a few with life sentences. Five blocks in total, one of which is for transgender."

Clayton is a small town about three miles away from Bradford on the road to Thornton, and the prison is about a mile from the entrance to the town. BWP's forensic team had already begun their investigation when the two detectives arrived at Clayton Prison.

“They found Diane Dunmore’s body in the library,” said Carol Thomas. “Is that Diane from the Dunmore family?”

“She was, indeed. As far as I recall, a kind of ‘black sheep’ of the family,” replied Gareth Donovan, looking for a suitable place to park the car.” I remember her, once she was one of the favourite victims of the local scandal newspapers. After finding this post at the library, she put herself in a shadowy area, she was probably considered uninteresting. Odd, isn’t it?”

“Is that so? Why would a girl like her want to work in such a lowly job? Why not work in the family company? Or even better, she could afford not to work at all.”

“She was a bit of a strange girl. A terrible teenager in the Dunmore family,” Gareth said. “The only child but a big trouble for poor parents. A few years ago, she married Chris Patterson, a well-known adventurer casanova looking for young women with money, according to the local gossip. He was an officer here in the prison, I understood. Huh, not that he could find a better environment for him, I think I met him once. Repulsive chap, I don’t really know what women could find in him. Anyway, Diane married him against her family’s approval. It didn’t take long for her to understand what a terrible mistake she had made. It is said he cheated on her and they had a formal marriage, each of them with his own life.”

Carol smiled indulgently. Gareth used to read all the newspapers every morning, including the tabloids. They already had gone through the access formalities and an officer offered to take them to the scene of the crime in the library.

The library and the education department were in a separate bungalow-style building about five minutes’ walk from the main gate, past the administration building and next to the five prisoner blocks (A, B, C, D, and E). The library was rectangular in shape, with one of the entrances on the small side through a massive wooden door doubled by a metal grill, both locked. On the right side of the room, there were seven parallel stands with books and the desk where Eleonor Wilson, librarian manager, worked. Next to it, three other, shorter stands, with DVDs with movies and CDs with music, arranged on shelves, thematically. Carol walked among the stands looking at the books with interest. Most were fiction, classic literature, and a few non-fiction including self-development books, motivational, cooking, and foreign languages course packs.

Eleonor Wilson's desk was full of books and DVDs, lots of papers were thrown into disarray and two computers, one of them was Eleonor's. At the opposite end of the entrance were two other small rooms. On the long side of the room was a door leading to the education department. Another door led to a room that appeared to be a workspace, with a small storage space where the body had been found. This room was larger with a rectangular table in the middle. On the table, plenty of books, papers, labels, and DVDs seemed to be in processing. The forensic team was quietly doing its job.

According to the first examination, Diane Dunmore had died the day before, between lunchtime and 5:00 pm and death was caused by strong blows to the head with a heavy object, possibly metal. Experts assumed that she was in the small storage room when she was hit as there were no signs that her body had been dragged from somewhere. Diane wore a pair of black fabric trousers, a black blouse, and a short brown jacket on top. Like all prison employees, she had a black leather belt and a small black pouch with a metal chain at the end of which dangled four keys, two massive and two smaller. The access card with a small photo was also attached to the belt. Only a pack of white tissues and a hand notebook were found in her pockets. A few pages had been torn in a hurry.

Experts had searched Diana's car, a black Mini Cooper, in the prison car park, inside which they had seen a textile bag containing a sandwich and several chocolate bars. They had not found Diane's mobile in the car. The body and her personal belongings had been removed, and the police team was doing the final investigations in the room where the victim was found.

Gareth was looking over the DVD stands.

"You know, Gareth, I'd love to work in a library, it's so quiet and peaceful," said Carol, examining the bookshelves.

"Huh! As you can see, it's not very quiet," replied Gareth. "Good movie collection, isn't it? I see some interesting classic movies here."

"Yes, it's not too bad. Let's see where we can set the workspace. We have to talk to the witnesses, I'd say to start with Eleonor Wilson, the library manager, what do you think? I understand she discovered the body."

"Not quite, it was Kristin Burton who discovered it. Eleonor Wilson was in the library as well. But I agree with you, I'm going to get her in here. She and her colleagues are waiting in the education department. Hopefully, they are better now after this unexpected trauma."

What Eleonor Wilson Says

Gareth came back promptly accompanied by Eleonor Wilson, who assured them she was fine. Carol studied her discreetly as she tried to warm her cold hands. Of medium height, wiry, without make-up, but with a neat appearance, Eleonor Wilson seemed to embody her idea of a classic librarian, with a low-key appearance and a neutral outfit. The hair, rich and slightly grey, was cut to the base of the neck and neatly combed with severe bangs across her high forehead. Her eyes, deep blue, had a tired and sad expression, but they exuded confidence and self-possession. The woman appeared to be in her middle 50s.

"Before answering your questions, would you like some tea or coffee to warm up?" She asked in an almost muffled voice. Gareth happily approved.

"A tea would be great," replied Carol gratefully. "Can you tell us how the library works and how you use all the rooms? And then, can we have a space where we can organise the interviews with the witnesses, please?"

Eleonor Wilson agreed with a soft smile and then explained to them professionally, "This is the main room of the library," she said soberly, "residents only have access here. The other three rooms are for staff only, and residents can have access in the presence of staff members. One of those three rooms is my office, with a computer, the one with an external connection. This is where I keep documents, forms, folders, correspondence, and other official papers. Next to my office, the small adjoining room is the *Carlton Room*, a work room, which we normally use for legal advice activities and Carlton Trust meetings with residents.

"Carlton Trust is a charity we work with that provides psychological and legal counselling for residents," Eleonor explained, seeing the curiosity on Gareth's face. "The third room, the *Harper Room*, the one where Diane was found, is larger and we use it to organise various events, workshops, clubs, you saw that there are several tables and chairs. In that storage room where Diane was found, we keep empty boxes, a trolley for moving heavy boxes, and other materials we use in the library that residents should not have access to, such as cutting or laminating tools. We also use *Harper Room* for processing and cataloguing new books, DVDs, and music CDs," pointed out Eleonor Wilson.

"Just you and the other two colleagues, Diane, and Kristin work there," Gareth said.

"Indeed. The residents are allowed only in the presence of one of us."

"Is the door usually locked?"

"Yes, it is, we usually keep it always locked. The locker has a flaw, it opens if not locked, either from the inside or the outside. When we work inside and to keep quiet, we must lock it from the inside with a small key. To be more explicit, there is a lot of noise when the residents come to the library. Then, they are tempted to go in if they see the door open. And steal things from there."

Gareth examined the door, trying not to disturb the team of experts inside. He noticed that it had no handle and could not be kept closed unless it was locked with one of the three keys, the small one.

"Why is this room so important?" Carol asked, intrigued.

"Mainly because we keep the new books and DVDs here that we are going to process and put into the library catalogue. We also have various other materials that must not reach the residents, the video camera, staplers, two cassette players, or various utensils, the laminating machine, for example."

"I saw there is another door in the back, can it be opened?" Carol asked.

"That door opens to the IT room, where the IT courses for the residents are held. But it's permanently locked, we never use it and the key is in my office in a drawer," said Eleonor.

"Could you check if the key is there, please?" Carol asked.

"Sure, come with me, please." Eleonor walked over to her desk and opened one of the metal cabinet drawers. He pulled out a black pouch with a string of keys. "Here it is," he said, showing them a white key. "It looks new, compared to the other used keys on the string."

"Does anyone else have this key?"

"No, just us. And, as I said, we don't use this door, so we keep it permanently locked."

" I see, we will check this door a bit later. Could you please explain how the library works, it's different to a public library, isn't it? How do you work with…readers?" Gareth asked.

"Of course. We have a set schedule for residents who come to the library. There are five blocks, and we have a time slot for each of them. For instance, on Mondays, from 9.00 to

9.45, there is a slot allocated to the residents of Block A. Sometimes we have two to three; sometimes we have 20 girls who come to the library to borrow books, DVDs, and music CDs. Mondays are always busy here."

"They come accompanied by officers, I presume?" Gareth asked.

"Yes, usually they are. The officers remain in the library and wait for the girls to return and pick out other materials that we process. Sometimes, the officers go into an adjoining room to the duty officer in the education department. They wait there until we finish processing the loans and come back to accompany the girls back to the block where they live."

"What usually does the duty officer in the education department do?" Gareth asked.

"He manages the groups that come to the department for classes and the library. They must resolve any incidents that occur during classes and then make sure that no one is left in the building at the final of the day. As a rule, after 6:00 pm, they check all the rooms and lock everything."

"I see, do they work in a rotation system or is there someone who works permanently?"

"No, they work on a rota system. Monday, I think it was Matthew but needs to be checked."

Gareth nodded and made a note in his notebook. Carol was poring over the schedule list.

"What does this education slot mean?" She asked.

"Well, every day, in the morning and in the afternoon, we have a time slot, 30 minutes, allocated to residents coming to the education department for courses. It doesn't matter what block they live in. They are allowed to pop into the library to bring and borrow materials without being brought by the officers. They come through the door that leads to the education department and keep going back there."

Eleonor led them into the *Carlton Room* and brought two large mugs of tea. Gareth sat down in one of the chairs and placed his notebook on the table in front of him.

"Could you tell us how yesterday went and when you last saw Diane Dunmore?" He asked.

"Yesterday was a quiet day," said Eleonor Wilson. "Nothing unusual with Diane, I asked her to process a new batch of DVDs received last week, three large boxes, in the Harper Room. We had residents from blocks A and C in the morning, about 20, but nothing problematic. I served, assisted by Grace, and everything was ok. Kristin came in the afternoon and the other orderly, Helen helped her then."

"Who is Grace?" Gareth asked.

"Oh, sorry, I forgot to mention it. We have two residents, Grace, and Helen, who work with us as my assistants. Yesterday, it was Grace in the morning and Helen after lunch."

"Do you trust them? How did you select them to work here?" Carol asked.

"They applied for the position of assistant librarian, and I interviewed each of them. Grace has been working with us for around five months, I think, I'll check. Helen has been here since last August; I am very pleased with them. They are really helpful in the library."

"You have access to their records, I presume. Do you know why they are here?" Gareth asked.

Eleonor nodded and said softly, "Yes, both girls are here for fraud, no risk for any of us. Besides, they are also highly motivated to do their job well and to receive positive references, which matters in the annual evaluation."

"How was Diane yesterday?" Gareth wanted to know.

Eleonor frowned slightly, to give a fair and precise response.

"She came at 8:30 yesterday, at the right time, I remember this detail because she is usually late. She was a little quiet and preoccupied, but I didn't ask her why; I know she had some problems in her marriage. I thought it was best to mind my business. I asked her to start processing the DVDs received last week, as I said. She wasn't too thrilled, I presume. Preferring to work with residents, processing loans. She was, I would say, a very communicative person. We discussed the schedule for the day. I told her that I had to leave around 1:30 pm, as I needed an afternoon off, and that she needed to finish processing the DVDs by the end of the day. Then I think she went to the education department for about 30 minutes, I don't know exactly what she did there.

"About 9:30, she went into the *Harper Room*, and I suppose she worked. I had two groups of residents and Grace helped me with them. Grace finished her work as usual at 11:30 and left the library, I think for her apartment. From noon, I worked in my office, reading my correspondence, and answering e-mails, but did not see Diane at all. I heard her go out a few times, but I didn't check what she was doing or where she was. It was a little after 1:00 pm when Diane and I went into the blocks to hand out some letters and collect the books from the return boxes."

"Return boxes, what are they exactly?" Gareth interrupted her.

"Each block has a plastic box where residents return the borrowed books or DVDs if they do not want to come to the library. These boxes are usually located near the duty officers' rooms in each block. They are locked and the keys are with me or Diane. It's just the two of us doing this operation, one day a week, usually on Mondays, at lunchtime, when the residents are in the cells. This is because residents put the books in the return boxes during the weekend when the library is closed."

"So, it's just you and Diane doing this? Were you together yesterday?" Carol asked.

"Yes, we left the library together around 1:15 pm, but I didn't accompany her to all the blocks. Only in B as I had to talk to a resident. Then I let Diane go to all the other blocks, get all the materials from the boxes. I left at 1:30 pm; she assured me that she was feeling confident enough to collect the books on her own. It was not the first time she had done this. That was the last time I saw Diane," Eleonor said softly. "I remember telling her that from 2:30 pm Kristin was due to come and her task was to process the loans for two groups in blocks D and E. I emphasised my request to Diane to finish processing the DVDs by the end of the day so that we can get them into the system today. She seemed a bit distracted to me but maybe I was wrong."

-"You left at 1:30 pm, you said. Did you pop into the library before, or head straight for the exit?" Carol asked.

"No, straight to the gate, I had taken my rucksack with me."

"I see," said Carol. "Diane continued to do this operation and then returned to the library. What happened next?"

"I really don't know, I just saw in the morning that she left behind the desk the boxes of books and DVDs collected from the blocks, and I assumed that everything was fine. This morning I arrived as usual a little after 8.00, I think it was 8.20 and started scanning the books Diane collected yesterday. Then came Kristin and you know the rest."

"You didn't go into the *Harper Room* this morning, did you? Was the door locked?" Carol asked.

"I didn't go in," answered Eleonor, "I didn't need to. Yes, the door was locked, everything seemed to be as usual. I would have noticed on arrival if it wasn't locked, I always check everything when I get here. I'm sure Kristin unlocked it when she went to get the trolley, but you should check this with her."

Carol carefully notes the details in her notebook.

"What key do you use to unlock this door?" She asked her.

Eleonor Wilson pointed to one of the three keys on her belt, the small one.

"This key unlocks *almost* all interior doors," she said.

"This means that any member of staff could have access here," said Carol

"Yes, indeed, any employee of the prison, including the officers," Eleonor approved.

"Same as in the storage room?"

"Likewise, indeed," Eleonor nodded again.

Carol thought it was very important to check with the security department the information about access to the keys.

"What can you tell us about Diane, was she a good colleague?" Gareth asked.

"Yes, I was pleased working with her. No incident, she got along well with the residents," answered Eleonor with a sad look.

"Who would want her dead, though? Did she have enemies here as far as you know?" Gareth insisted.

" No one, as far as I am aware. She was on good terms with all her colleagues, I haven't heard of any argument answered Eleonor with a tired expression. However, I think that her husband was a bit of a trouble, colleagues say that he was not exactly the perfect husband. Maybe Kristin would tell you more," Eleonor added impliedly.

Gareth and Carol looked at each other to check if they both noticed the same hint from Eleonor's voice.

"Any idea about how long will the library be closed?" Eleanor Wilson asked. "I'll have to let the residents know we're closed and decide what to do for the next few days."

"I do not know exactly, let's see when my colleagues will finish their investigation here. We'll let you know as soon as we have information," Gareth replied. "In the coming days, we will also have to speak to the two residents, Helen Evans, and Grace Davies, could you help us set up discussions with them?"

"Sure, I will also talk to Mary, you have my full support. When do you want to talk to the girls?"

"Tomorrow morning, would that be possible? In one of the available rooms here," Gareth replied.

"Perfect, I'll let you know about the time right away. Do you want to talk to Kristin now, shall I tell her to come over?"

"Yes, please, we're waiting for her here. One more thing," Carol said. "What are the library opening hours?"

“We work from 8:30 am to 5:00 pm. Opening hours with residents, however, are between 9:30 am and 4:30 pm.”

“But never after 4:30 pm?”

“No, the girls must return to the blocks at 4:30 pm.”

“I see, thank you very much for your information,” Gareth said. “And for the tea as well, very timely indeed.”

“No worries. You can find me at the education department if you need me,” Eleonor said and headed for the door.

What Kristin Burton Says

Gareth turned to Carol with a curious look.

"Well, what do you think about Eleonor Wilson?" He asked.

"Too soon to say, you know I don't go by first impressions. What do we know about husband Chris Patterson? Was he informed of Diane's death?"

"Yes, he was notified, apparently, he was on duty at Clayton's yesterday after dinner and last night. They called him at home, we'll have to pay him a visit later."

Kristin Burton entered the room and sat silently in a chair in front of the two detectives.

"How do you feel, Kristin, are you better now, can you talk about what happened this morning?" Carol asked sympathetically.

"I am fine now, but it was a nightmare. Not a good way to start the week for sure. I do not see a dead body every day, that's right," answered the woman with a sad absent smile.

Kristin was tall and slim with rich brown hair in large messy curls. The brown eyes had a distant expression and Carol noticed the deep wrinkles on her high forehead, maybe a sign that life had not brought her much joy. However, she did not appear to be more than 40 years old. She was wearing a dark green jacket with a loose cut and a mid-length cherry-coloured dress.

"True, and you reacted very well. Please tell us, when was the last time you saw Diane?"

"Sure. It was yesterday. I arrived after lunch, a little after 2:00 pm, maybe 2:20 pm, I can't remember exactly. I worked at Eleonor's desk starting with the first group of residents who came at 2:30 pm. Eleonor instructed me last Friday that I was going to process the loans. Diane was busy with the new books and DVDs in the *Harper Room*. We haven't seen each other at all. One of our orderlies, Helen came on time, it was 2:30 pm I think, and we worked together until 4:30 pm when we finished the program. I then left. I only work part-time, Diane is, was, actually, full-time, as was Eleonor."

"You didn't see her yesterday, did you?"

"That is correct, indeed. But I assumed, however, that she was there. Our morning orderly, Grace, confirmed for me when I arrived. She had come from the education department around 2:00 pm. Diane had unlocked the door for her and let her into the library. Grace was looking for a book for another resident and was waiting for someone to let her go as at 2.30 was *free movement*."

"What is *free movement*?" Carol interrupted her.

"When the gate between the blocks and the education department and other administrative buildings is open. There are four *free movement* slots every day, at 9:30, 11:30, 2:30 and 4:30 for 10 minutes only. Residents can move from blocks to administrative buildings and back. It is especially for the residents who are working or studying. It is to help them get on time to their jobs, I mean."

"I see," Carol said. "What next?"

"As I said, I got here around 2.20 and I found Grace in the library. She said that she must go to the gym. I unlocked the library door and let her go after talking a little. Grace told me that Diane was working in the *Harper Room* processing new DVDs and didn't want to be disturbed, especially by me."

"Why especially you?" Gareth asked.

Kristin looked at him coldly and replied, "You will probably find out sooner or later, Chris, Diane's husband, and I have been in a serious relationship for almost a year, we want to get married. Diane knew and was going to divorce him, I think she never loved him, they only got married because she wanted to annoy her family who she loathed. At least that's what Chris thinks. In the end, we tried to avoid each other as much as possible. Eleonor knew that."

"You assumed that Diane was working in the *Harper Room*. Was the door open?" Carol asked.

"The door was closed, of course. The library was noisy, and Diane used to keep it locked, sometimes the girls were tempted to get in if they saw the door open. It's stressful watching them not get their hands on something. I did not pay too much attention, anyway; I was in a hurry. I had to switch the computer on and prepare for the coming groups."

"I see," said Carol. "Did Diane come out of the *Harper Room,* or did you see anyone go in there while you were working?"

"While I was serving at the desk, I don't remember her going out, but I was busy with the residents, I didn't pay attention. I don't remember anyone coming in. However, I'd been out a few times, I'd been a little in the education department and in the toilet, when they weren't resident in the library, of course."

"The two access doors to the library, I mean, the one from the main entrance and the other to the education department are permanently locked, aren't they?"

Kristin strongly confirmed.

"Definitely. It's one of the prison rules, not sure if you know about it. Unlock, enter, and lock back. You have probably been told how keys are used. Without keys, you are stuck, you cannot get in, you cannot get out."

"Sure," said Carol, "we will talk to security about the keys." She recalled that Diane had a belt and a set of four keys when she was found dead.

"When was the last time you saw Diane?" Gareth asked.

"It was Friday afternoon for sure, at the summary meeting. It was, as usual, nothing special. We didn't exchange a word, she ignored me, and so did I. At that meeting, Eleonor discussed with us the next week's library agenda. It was short, about 20 minutes. We finished at nearly 4:30 pm and I was off."

"What do you think about Diane, did she have enemies, who would want her dead?" Carol asked.

"Diane was a toxic person, she liked to dig and find out people's dirty secrets and have fun at their expense. I think she misguided her career to come here, she didn't have the slightest interest in literature or libraries in general. And she was not capable of compassion. She just enjoyed talking to the residents and gossiping."

"Did she have close friends among colleagues or residents?" Gareth asked.

"I didn't see that she had. But she got along better with some residents, like Helen and Grace. At one time, she had grown close to Deborah, but the poor woman had a heart attack a few months ago."

"This morning, when you entered the *Harper Room*, can you recall if the door was locked?" Carol asked.

"Yes, it was locked, I remember precisely. And the storage room door, too. Otherwise, it would have caught my attention. Eleonor told us to always keep them locked, it's safer."

"Did you notice anything unusual in the *Harper Room*?"

"Nothing, I saw the boxes with DVDs and DVD cases scattered on the table. I went in to get the trolley from the storage room. Eleonor had asked me to go to the main gate to get some packages of newspapers from there and I needed the trolley. We always use the trolley to bring packages from the main gate, they are too heavy. Then I saw her in a corner."

Kristin stopped and glared at the two detectives. She looked tired and clearly needed a break.

"We should stop here, but we stay in touch, of course. Maybe you should talk to Eleanor Wilson and go home, it's been very difficult for you today," Gareth said and handed her a business card.

"Please call us if you remember anything, any detail may be of interest," he said.

Kristin thanked them and said that she might go home. Gareth glanced at his watch and then checked his interview notes.

"We didn't have too much, but it's only the first day," said Carol thoughtfully. "We should go to the security department. We need to understand how they use the access keys and see what we can find out from their CCTV cameras."

An Interesting Chat at the Prison Security Department

Carol and Gareth left the library with the distinct feeling that they were being followed. It was already lunch time, and the prison staff were getting ready for their lunch break. Beyond the gates, an intense tumult with the female prisoners chatting heatedly in small groups. Some of them carried textile bags on their shoulders, they were returning from their temporary jobs or classes in the education department. There were some little round tables in the courtyard and some girls were sitting playing cards or laughing loudly.

Carol and Gareth made their way to the administration building where they assumed the security department was located. At the entrance, they were greeted by a tall and very jovial officer who led them directly to the manager of the security department. John Pritchet welcomed them into his office with a courteous and amiable smile, though it was obvious that he would have preferred the meeting to take place after lunchtime.

"I heard about what happened to Diane Dunmore, poor girl, it's horrible, nothing like this has happened since I've been here for 18 years. I am at your disposal if you need information."

"You are very kind, can you explain how the key access system works, please? It can help us a lot in the investigation," Gareth said and placed the belt and the chain with the four keys, found on Diana's body, on the table.

"Sure, it's no problem. All staff members must wear a belt with a holder of three keys, two are from the external gates and the third key unlocks almost all the inward doors."

"So, without keys, you can't move in the prison."

"That's right, you can't get in, you can't get out. It is a prison," said Pritchet smiling.

He looked carefully at the keys found at Diane's and said in surprise, "This set of keys belongs to the officers. Where did you find them?"

"Those were found on Diane, she had them when she was discovered."

"That's odd, she was supposed to have a set of keys for the staff. Officers have a different set than staff. And they are kept in separate cabinets. I will have to report this incident," he said thoughtfully.

"What is the difference between the keys worn by the staff and those for the officers?" Carol asked.

"They are the same basically. The two large keys are for the gates and the little one is for the inward doors. But officers have a set of four keys, meaning they have an extra key, the one that opens the prisoners' cells. Staff members do not have access to this fourth key. As I said, the staff has two keys for the gate and a third key, the small one, for the inward doors."

"Can you show us where you keep the keys and how to access them?" Carol asked.

"Sure, come with me, please," said Pritchett conceitedly.

He led them down a corridor, into a room next to the main entrance to the prison. The room had on one of the walls two large wooden cabinets with holders for sets of three keys for the members of staff. Each holder had a number on top and a small light bulb that turned red when the set of keys was removed. The light turned blue after the key set was put back in the holder. On another wall, there were three more large wooden cabinets with keys for officers, the security manager explained to them.

"Each member of staff must take, upon arrival, a set of three keys from one of these two cabinets, it is a secured system. Access to the set of keys is based on a password that should be typed on a small monitor placed under the handle of each cabinet. Both staff and officers receive the password at the entrance, based on their personal access permit. Passwords change daily. Each set of keys is assigned a single numbered holder, so you cannot put another key in there. Please see, the holder number is put on a small key ring next to the keys so that the employees know where to put the set when they leave, I mean in the exact same holder. No one can leave the prison with the keys, the cameras at the entrance signal if the employee has failed to return them."

"Do you check if everyone has put keys in the cabinets?"

"We do. Every evening, after 6:30 pm, we check if the prison staff have put the keys back into their cabinets. As I said, the officers have different cabinets and the lack of keys in the holder does not alarm us, they are taken by the officers on duty during the night. With the staff instead, it is different, all keys must be in their holders by 6:30. They usually do not stay after the end of the program. As a rule, those who stay after this time must notify the duty officer at reception. A missing key from the holder would trigger the alarm, no one can leave, and the investigation begins."

"My understanding is that the lack of the set of keys taken by Diane from the officers' cabinet did not alarm the security department. If she had keys from the cabinet assigned to the staff, the lack of keys would trigger the alarm and the security department would start the investigation. Am I right?"

"Yes, that's right," confirmed Pritchett.

"Members of staff don't have access to officers' keys and vice versa, is that correct?"

"Exactly. There are two different passwords, for staff and for officers. Unless, say, they know the password for the cabinet," replied Pritchet.

"How do they get the passwords?" Carol asked.

"At the entrance, they must swipe the access card and the password is displayed on the small screen of the entrance scanner only for a few seconds. They must memorise it and type it then in the monitors of the cabinets."

"Can you find out if Diane took a different set of keys than the one, we discovered with her, I mean the one here?" Carol asked, pointing to the set of keys they had brought with them.

"Unfortunately, we can't say that as we don't know which key each employee took. We can only know if these keys are returned in time to their slots."

Carol resignedly nodded. She then asked if they could learn about the monitoring system in the library and see the CCTV cameras near the library.

"Of course, I can lead you to my colleague who manages the monitoring and access activity in the prison departments," said the manager promptly. The thought of being free to eat his lunch in peace seemed to bring him satisfaction. He conducted them down another corridor to a large room with a dozen computers and lots of plastic cables. A tattooed young man was working intently at a screen. He was carrying earphones and didn't even notice their presence.

"Daniel," the manager shouted, "detectives Carol Thomas and Gareth Donovan are from *Bradford West Police* and they want to know more about the CCTV monitoring system in the library. They want to see yesterday's CCTV footage. You know about the murder in the library, please give them all the information they are interested in."

"Sure," said the young man cheerfully.

Carol and Gareth thanked the manager, who assured them of his full availability for further information and hurried away.

"Ok, Daniel," Gareth said with a fatherly tone, "what can you tell us about the CCTV cameras in the library? We are interested in finding out whether and where Diane Dunmore went yesterday after 1:00 pm."

"Let's see," said the young man, searching feverishly through the files on the computer. "The library has a CCTV camera in the main hall that basically monitors access to the library through the main door and the office."

"Aren't there others in the library rooms?"

"No, only this one in the main room where the prisoners have access."

Half an hour later, Carol and Gareth were walking out the prison gate and heading towards the car park where they had left their car on arrival.

"I'd say let's go get something to eat, we skipped lunch time today," Gareth said, looking at the clock. It was nearly two o'clock. "We put our thoughts and notes in order."

"Good idea, Gareth, I was waiting for you to say that. I'm starving. We have enough time. At four o'clock, we must get to Chris Patterson's house on Tumbling Hill Street."

It was an ordinary November day with a leaden sky. Gareth drove quietly and parked the car on Listerhill Road near the *Mitre* pub where they stopped to eat before heading to Tumbling Hill Street.

"What do we have so far?" Gareth summarised after they finished eating and having a steaming coffee in front of them. "On Tuesday, 12 November, around 8:45 am, the body of 27-year-old woman, Diane Dunmore, is discovered in a library room at Clayton Prison, where she had worked for nearly two years. The body is discovered by her colleague, Kristin Burton, who, in fact, is the mistress of her husband, Chris Patterson. The coroner's preliminary report said Diane Dunmore had died the day before, between 12:30 and 5:00 pm, from severe blows to the head with a heavy object. The murder weapon has not yet been discovered.

"The body was discovered in the storage room of the library, to which all prison employees had access. According to the description of their boss, Eleanor Wilson, manager librarian, the day before, Diane came to work on time and had to process a new set of DVDs and books in the *Harper Room*. After 1:00 pm, Diane left the library, accompanied by Eleanor Wilson, to collect the books and DVDs from the return boxes in several blocks of the prison. This procedure takes place every Monday between 1:00 and 2:00 when the prisoners are in their cells and the officers change shifts. According to the

CCTV cameras, at 1:20 pm, Eleonor and Diane left the library and headed towards Block B. They left 10 minutes later, at 1:30 pm to be exact, when Eleonor headed for the exit gate, the cameras confirmed her statement.

"At 1:46 pm, Diane was on her way to Block A, where she stayed for 10 minutes. She went out with a box full of books, went back to the library to empty the box and came out again with an empty box heading towards Block C. At 1:57, she entered the library with the last box full of books, then it was last seen alive. We can assume that Diane was killed between 1:57 pm and 5:00 pm. At 2:20 pm, Kristin arrived at the library and began work with the afternoon orderly, Helen. Kristin Burton did not meet Diane but assumed she was in the Harper Room. Grace Davies, the morning orderly, had told her that Diane Dunmore worked there, and she did not want to be disturbed. Diane and Kristin were not on very good terms; no wonder they worked separately.

"Helen left the library at 4:25 through the door to the education department. At 4:35 pm, Kristin locked up and left without checking if Diane was still in the library. Diane Dunmore used to work full-time so she should finish the program at 5:00 pm. The CCTV does not show Diane Dunmore leaving the library. The light was turned off by the duty officer from the education department at 6:30 pm after making sure that no one was left in the library. We need to talk to him," he said and made a note in his notebook.

"The next morning, Kristin accidentally discovered Diana Dunmore's body in the Harper Room. According to her statement, both the doors to the storage room and the entrance to the *Harper Room* were locked."

“ We need to find out more about what happened yesterday, after 1:57 pm,” Carol said. “We should talk to the two orderlies, Grace and Helen, they can give us important information. But first, let’s talk to Chris Patterson.”

What Husband Chris Patterson Says

It was nearly 4:00 pm when the detectives parked the car in front of the number 13 house on Tumbling Hill Street, belonging to Diane Dunmore and Chris Patterson. It was a massive Victorian house with tall windows and walls partially covered with ivy. The courtyard was spacious and well-kept, with magnolias and roses, and two paths led one to the main entrance, the other somewhere behind the house. Chris Patterson greeted them at the door with a tired and sad look. Two long brown circles were visible under his swollen eyes.

"Please come in, I was waiting for you. I was on night duty and this terrible news overwhelmed me." A terrier greeted them with a friendly bark. "Terry, come here," the man said, and the dog gladly obeyed.

Chris Patterson was tall and athletic, with brown hair and well-defined black eyebrows. He exuded an air of confidence and insolence, despite the weariness that seemed to mark his tanned and prematurely wrinkled face. Patterson seemed to be in his late 40s.

Patterson invited them into a small and cosy lounge next to the entrance and offered them a drink. An empty glass and a nearly full bottle of whiskey were on a side table.

On the mantel, two framed photographs, one of Diane, the other from their wedding. *Quite a good-looking couple*, Carol thought. She looked closely at Diane's photo. *Diane had not been a beautiful woman*, she thought, *but she had a provocative look and exuded an overflowing sexuality.* Of medium height, with long, lean legs, she was the type who could not have gone unnoticed. Long and rich hair, a natural blonde. Long face with strong jaws and a big eagle-like nose that made Carol think of a bird of prey. Her eyes instead were extremely beautiful, light green, almond-shaped with a daring and sensual expression. Quite a remarkable look, Carol thought.

"Terrible news, I didn't expect it," said Chris, and poured himself whiskey from the opened bottle.

"When did you last see Diane?" Carol asked.

"It was yesterday morning before she headed to Clayton. I was on the afternoon shift. I didn't leave until lunch at Clayton. But I had to get up early to take Terry for a walk."

"How was she like then?"

" She was as usual. The day before we had discussed about Terry, we had to take him to the vet, for the vaccine. We delayed a lot."

"Did you get along well?" Carol asked and gazed at him.

Chris sat down in the armchair in front of them and said distantly, "It's not a secret now; we were going to divorce, she wanted to be free. To be honest, I never understood Diane, she was a strange person. She was not attached to anything, only to herself."

"Would you say that you did not have a happy marriage?"

"Diane only married me because she knew her family didn't want me. She enjoyed it a lot to cause them trouble, I don't understand why, an unhappy childhood perhaps. I had a feeling it was something that had happened in her childhood, but I didn't try to find out. My life was complicated enough. She asked me for divorce saying that she wanted to start a new life by herself."

"Oh," said Carol, "did she meet someone?"

"Have no idea. I told you. She was a strange person. I never truly knew what was in her head. I don't know anything about her life, in a way. Moreover, we were living separately for two years. Me with my life, she with hers, and believe me, it wasn't simple."

"What do you mean?" Gareth asked.

"Diane had her own demons from the past, but she didn't share anything with me, she believed I was not able to understand. At least that's what she said, she didn't care for me at all."

"Is it true that you have a relationship with her colleague, Kristin Burton?" Gareth asked again.

"Yes, we've been seeing each other for a while, it is true," Chris agreed with a wry smile.

"What did Diane say?"

"She didn't care too much. She didn't even like her, saying Kristin was awkward."

"Who will inherit Diane's fortune?" Carol asked curtly, trying to catch Patterson's eye expression.

"No idea, to be honest. I will speak to Henry, the family lawyer, at the appropriate time."

"Do you know if Diane had a will?"

"If she had, she never mentioned it to me. She was perfectly healthy anyway, and death was the last thing on her mind," Chris said staring blankly.

“How did she decide to work at the prison library?” Gareth asked.

“She got hired about two years ago, I suppose. Her uncle worked there many years ago, Brian Dunmore. Not sure whether you’ve heard of him, he passed away last year.”

Gareth smacked himself lightly across the forehead. Yes, how could he have forgotten, that’s right, he remembered Brian Dunmore, over 60, had died of a cocaine overdose.

“How did she get along with her colleagues? Did she have someone close to her in prison?” Carol asked.

“Diane had no friends, only interests,” said Chris with a sly wink.

“What do you mean, what interests did she have?”

“I think that Diane was chasing a subject, doing some personal investigation into a prison corruption case. She said absolutely nothing to me, but she was very feverish and excited about her findings. Did you know that she used to work at a tabloid during university? Apparently, she liked dirty secrets and took great pleasure in learning the dark side of people’s lives. She lived for these,” Chris said as a grey shadow spread over his face.

“You have no idea who was Diane chasing or what the subject was?” Carol asked.

“No, honestly, Diane never told me anything, for the simple reason that she didn’t trust me. She used to write daily and make notes on her laptop.”

“Do you know if she took it with her yesterday when she left?” Carol asked.

“Yes, I think so, she took it, she always took it with her and left it in the car during the day. We are not allowed to take laptops or phones inside the prison, of course. Then I saw that she had it yesterday in the morning in the living room when she had her coffee. She was reading something when I saw her before I went out with Terry," Patterson answered confidently.

"Okay. Can you tell us about how your workday ran yesterday?" Gareth asked.

"Nothing unusual, my afternoon shift was from 12:00 to 6:00. Then, I came home to walk Terry for about an hour, then met Kristin at the *Hedgehog and Rabbit* for dinner. I got back to Clayton for the night shift, at about 8:30, I think. I actually did Rob's shift last night. I started at 9:00, until 3:00 in the morning."

"Tell us about the afternoon shift, something unusual, what exactly did you do?" Gareth insisted.

"I had to finish some reports in the administrative block until almost 1:30 pm when I had to bring two groups of residents from blocks A and D to the education department."

"Do you remember how long it took?"

"I accompanied a group of five girls to the math class, before 2:00 pm, at 1:30 pm, I don't know exactly. I left them in the class and then went to Block D. I talked a little with Jackson in the office. I brought the second group around 2:00 I think, not sure. I left them at the hairdresser's class, with Laura, the hairdresser. Then I left the education department building, maybe before 2:10."

"What happened next?" Gareth asked.

"I popped into the gym to try out the new machines but Julie and Arnold, the instructors, were not there, so I worked out a bit by myself. At 3:00, I returned to the education department to take the two groups back to blocks A and D. First, it was the group from math class, then the second group from the hairdresser salon. We are not allowed to mix the groups. From 4:00 to 6:00, I was on duty in Block B, on the second floor, you can check."

"You hadn't seen Diane during the day, had you?"

"No, I was in the education department, but I didn't go to the library. I had no business there."

"So, between 2:10 and 3:00, you were in the gym. Were you there with anyone?"

"You mean if someone saw me if I have an alibi?" Patterson asked sarcastically.

Gareth didn't answer and Patterson rubbed his chin with a concerned air.

"Julie and Arnold came after a while, but I don't remember exactly, maybe after about 30 minutes," he said.

Gareth made meticulous notes and glanced briefly at his colleague.

Carol got up from her chair and asked permission to have a look in his wife's room. Patterson agreed and led them upstairs to Diane's room.

"She moved into this room more than a year ago, after an argument. As I said we had separate lives. Please, you can have a look," Chris said, making way for them to enter Diane's room. "It's just as Diane let it yesterday morning before she left."

Diane's room was large and bright, rectangular, with three tall, curtained windows. The room was obviously in the best position in the house. On one of the walls, a few abstract paintings, and a large desk in one part of the room, full of papers, magazines, and books in great disarray. Next to it was the fireplace and a small buffet with bottles of wine and whiskey and a few clean glasses. On the opposite side, a four-poster double bed, a few blouses and pairs of trousers were carelessly discarded in a hurry. *Diane was clearly far from a neat person*, Gareth thought disapprovingly. A large old mirror, next to the bedside table full of cosmetics and make-up kits. On the opposite side, a door led to a light and airy bathroom with a tall window and a round bathtub in the middle. A few pots of aloe vera plants made the bathroom warm and cosy.

Carol stopped and looked up at the paintings. One of them, depicting a stylised iris with thin, delicate petals, was mesmerising. Carol found it fascinating. A violet iris gliding on the waves of a murky river. The artist seemed to have found a stunningly beautiful colour for the iris, both a vivid and sad colour, highly contrasting with the grey waves of the river. The painting was gorgeous, but it exuded a sadness of great depth. Carol looked up at the two initials at the bottom: *IC*.

"Beautiful painting," Carol remarked thoughtfully, then turned to Gareth who was looking through the papers on the desk. "Diane wasn't very tidy, was she, Gareth?"

"You are indulgent," Gareth smiled. "What a bloody mess! But have you noticed something, there are no photos, family, friends, husband, nothing…" Gareth said. "People usually hold photos of family and friends in their personal rooms, but Diane has nothing."

"Aha, I couldn't explain what was unusual, the room was quite neutral, no memories, no past," Carol added.

They found no laptop or mobile, confirming the husband's assumption that Diane had them with her when she left for work. These had not, however, been found by investigators in Diane's car. This led to the conclusion that either the killer had taken them from the car or Diane had left them somewhere else before going to the prison library. The second option was quite unlikely, however.

Gareth took notes in his notebook and then glanced out the window. Beautiful house, a beautiful view. *Such a shame they were not happy*, he thought. Carol briefly inspected the wardrobe near the bathroom. Lots of brightly coloured day dresses and suits all indicated an active social life.

"Diane used to pay a lot of attention to her outfit," Chris explained, "but since she had taken a job at the prison library, she neglected herself."

"I see," said Carol, "do you think she regretted her past lifestyle?"

"I don't think so, she seemed excited with her life," answered Chris. "I would say that she really enjoyed working there. Not with the books," he added, "but with the girls. As I said, she was fascinated by their life stories."

"How did she get along with her colleagues?" Gareth asked.

Chris frowned and answered ambiguously, "She deeply despised Eleanor, saying she was conformist, limited and unable to do anything but scan books. Probably Eleonor, for her part, thought Diane was a frivolous woman and totally unsuitable for the job as a librarian. But they didn't have any major conflicts. At least, nothing that I was aware of," Chris said.

"Did Diane enjoy working with the female prisoners?" Carol asked.

" Yes, for sure. She said they were much more interesting than her colleagues," Chris said with a short laugh.

"In what sense?" Carol insists.

"I don't know exactly, I suspect she was referring to their stories, to life in prison probably, as I was saying."

Carol looked closely at Chris Patterson. *Surely, he knew something more, but he didn't want to say it*, she thought.

The two detectives thought that was enough for the moment and got up from the couch.

"That chap is not so repulsive as you suggested," said Carol when they got in the car

"Huh! I was sure you would say that. You women! Anyway, I feel like he is hiding something from us, I don't trust him."

Carol smiled sympathetically and closed the car door. They headed for the police headquarters, each with his own thoughts.

A Chat with the Dunmore Family's Lawyer

The next day it was almost 11:30 as they approached Clayton Prison. Carol had a meeting this morning with the Dunmore family's lawyer, Henry Watson, to find out details about Diane's potential will.

"Watson met me quite quickly," she told Gareth. "He said that Diane's relationship with her parents was quite distant, apparently, they never accepted her marriage to Patterson, they said he was an adventurer with no future, a fortune hunter. A few weeks ago, Diane phoned Watson to tell him she wanted to divorce."

"Aha, finally she took the right decision. What did you find out about the will, did she have one?" Gareth asked curtly.

"It seems not. Guess who is the heir?" Carol said.

"Well, do not tell me that could be Chris Patterson," Gareth replied ironically.

"Quite right. And it's not just about the house, listen. Diane owned 35% of the shares in the Dunmore family company. Looks like your friend, Patterson is rich now, he could live comfortably without any job."

"A perfect reason for a murder, don't you think?" Gareth said enthusiastically. "Then the house is worth at least two million pounds. Let me tell you what Peter Saunders told me."

Peter Saunders was one of Gareth's old colleagues and friends; they had known each other since university. Saunders ran *Business York*, a local newspaper. He had excellent local connections, knew the Dunmores well and knew all the gossip in town.

"Daniel Dunmore, Diane's father, runs the family business, *Agmore Company*, dealing with energy drinks and bottled spring water. It seems to be profitable and very well listed on the London Stock Exchange. Diane was an only child. Dan Dunmore also has a brother, Brian Dunmore, and a sister, Kathryn Dunmore, both of whom own percentages of the company's stock, as did Diane. Brian Dunmore died about a year ago and left Diane his share of the company. Brian was found dead in his home in *Covern Country* and investigations revealed that the cause of death was a cocaine overdose. At that time, an investigation was carried out, police believed he was involved in a drug and prostitution network that was connected to Clayton Prison. But they had no evidence to prove it. Police did not proceed with the investigation as Dan Dunmore intervened and the case was closed. Diane was already employed at Clayton Prison at that time."

"Interesting," said Carol. "What did Saunders say, how did Diane get along with her uncle?"

"Saunders didn't know too much. Anyway, he spoke to me not very nicely about her. According to him, Diane was not a brilliant journalist, she had no writing talent, but she was a good investigative reporter. She apparently loved being at the centre of local scandals. She despised her family and would do anything to cause them trouble—drunkenness, scandals, trouble with the local police. She was detained several times for indecent exposure and anti-social behaviour. Uncle Dunmore stepped in and helped her every time and apparently had some influence over her."

"Hm, interesting," said Carol thoughtfully again.

"About Patterson, Saunders confirmed what I have already told you. A dishonest and sordid guy. Crappy past and lots of women in his life. He likes to gamble and runs up debts that Diane used to pay off. They used to argue quite often, and the neighbours can confirm it."

"Scandalous couple," said Carol and checked her watch while she saw the prison building.

They parked the car and hurried up to the main gate of Clayton Prison.

A Short Visit to the Education Department

The education department was next to the library and seemed to be very popular with the female prisoners. Along a narrow corridor were placed nine classrooms, including mathematics, English, foreign languages, gastronomy, IT and hairdressing. At the end was a small secretariat and manager's office. Carol and Gareth stopped by the door marked *Mary Thomson, Manager* and pressed the bell, which rang briefly and loudly. Mary Thomson was a tall, stocky woman with a broad smile. She examines them over her glasses and invites them to sit in two armchairs located in front of her large desk.

"I was thinking that you would like to talk," she told them. "How can I help you?"

"Can you tell us a bit about Diane Dunmore? How was she like?"

"Diane was a good, empathic person, she often came here; she got along with Clare, my assistant, I guess. I don't know much about her. Anyway, Eleonor can tell you more. As far as I noticed, Diane was very sociable, she liked to talk to girls, listen to them and discuss their problems. Furthermore, she was running very well Carlton *Trust* project."

"What exactly does this project consist of?" Gareth wanted to know.

"I suppose that Eleonor also told you. *Carlton Trust* is a charity that provides legal advice and psychological training for residents. Diane was running this project well keeping track of consulting hours and preparing lists, doing evaluation reports. She sometimes made recommendations or suggested residents to be trained by the *Carlton Trust* for mentoring."

"What is mentoring?" Gareth asked.

"*Carlton Trust* works with a group of residents, they call them mentors, whose role is to support other prisoners with major problems—suicidal tendencies, drug, or alcohol addiction. It is not simple and if they have positive results, these mentors can receive good recommendations from the Carlton Trust which may persuade the assessment commissions to propose shortening the detention. They could be important to companies that employ ex-prisoners, of course."

"I see, so these assessments could be very important to the prisoners," Gareth said thoughtfully.

"Yes, but I repeat, they must have had notable results."

"And Diane could recommend residents for this training?"

"Yes, she could indeed, she and Eleonor. Because, through their activity in the library, they get to know the residents well."

Gareth nodded and made some notes in his notebook.

"Do you remember the last time you saw Diane?" Carol asked.

Mary Thomson strokes her chin gently with her right hand, trying to remember.

"It must have been last week, but I don't remember precisely. We met in the corridor, I was going to a meeting and she was talking to Laura, the instructor from the hairdressing course. We greeted each other, I noticed that she had lost a little weight, but she looked good."

"How did she get along with her colleagues in the library?"

"She wasn't too happy to work there, I perceived. But I don't know more. I think they were different personalities, but they worked well and that was the most important thing for me. In fact, Diane and Kristin, colleagues said, are not on good terms and it is because of Diane's husband, Officer Patterson. I don't know if it was true, just rumours, of course. Eleonor Wilson could be a little difficult, she is a hard-working person, not easy to work with, but I know that she loves her job very much, that's for sure. Kristin has been employed for a few months, part-time; she is a very discreet person, I don't know anything about her. Eleonor has been working here for a while, more than 15 years, I guess."

"Could we talk to your assistant too?" Gareth asked.

"Sure, I think she's in the secretariat," said Mary Thomson, delighted to have escaped interrogation.

Carol and Gareth thanked her and headed for the exit.

Clare Peter was in the secretariat and greeted them joyfully.

"I was shocked yesterday to hear what happened to my dear Diane. Monday morning, she was here; we had a coffee together. We usually have a little chat in the morning before classes start. I told her about Jan, my husband, who got fined for speeding. I was very annoyed, and she listened to me patiently."

“What do you think about Diane?”

“An excellent colleague for sure,” said Clare, “but she wasn’t too happy to work with her colleagues in the library, especially Eleonor. I hope this remains between us, please,” said Clare blinking at them. “They disliked each other, I think, but they had to work together.”

“How did she get along with Kristin?” Gareth asked impliedly.

“Ah, I see what you mean. Actually, Kristin’s relationship with Chris was no longer a secret here. Diane said she didn’t love her husband, that was for sure, and they had separate lives. Diane even told me that she was going to divorce soon. Both agreed to get a divorce.”

“Why did she decide to divorce right now, did she tell you? Any special reason?”

“We weren’t that close. I haven’t seen any change in her lately though, I doubt she’s met anyone though.”

“What exactly did you talk about on Monday?”

“As I was saying, I told her about Jan’s fine; I was very upset. She tried to comfort me, but it was clear that she was a bit thinking about something else. She was bored because she had to work on some books and DVDs recently purchased by the library. She enjoyed serving at the desk and processing loans. The girls liked her, I think more than Eleonor or Kristin. She laughed and talked with them. Eleonor and Kristin are not very talkative. I mean, they are doing their job without any sort of personal involvement.”

“I see what you mean. About how long did Diane stay with you?”

"About half an hour, I think. Mary called and asked me for some reports, I had to look them up on the computer and Diane left."

"Did you see each other again after that?"

"No, that was the last time I saw her, my dear little girl… Then, yesterday morning, Kristin burst into Mary's office with the terrible news that she had been found dead in the library."

"Do you think this crime could have been committed by one of the prisoners?"

Clare thought for a moment.

"I doubt that anyone would have wanted her dead, I don't understand. But everything is possible, some have mental problems. I wouldn't rule out any possibility," Clare said hesitantly.

"Let us know if you remember any details, whatever it may be."

"Sure, count on me."

Carol and Gareth thanked her for the information and headed for the library. The corridor was crowded with residents going in and out of the classrooms, talking and joking with the officers.

What the Orderlies Grace and Helen Say

Eleonor Wilson looked more relaxed than the previous day. She led them into the *Carlton Room* and told them that Grace Davies would be brought in by an officer in a few minutes.

Grace Davies was in her mid-30s, of medium height, slim, with shoulder-length brown hair combed simply back. She was wearing a pair of jeans and a green, short t-shirt that showed off her slim waist. The large blue eyes were melancholy, giving off a strong sense of fragility. She put rose lipstick on her very sensual lips. The officer told her to come in and she complied with unsteady steps.

"Grace Davies? Please, have a seat," Carol indicated the chair in front of her.

"Did you hear that Diane Dunmore was found dead in the library? We would like to speak to those who knew her," Gareth said gently.

"Yes, I heard, I feel for Diane, I was really shocked," Grace said in a shaky voice.

"Did you work well with her in the library?" Carol asked.

"Yes, I did. She was a brilliant colleague," Grace said looking sadly at the floor.

"Can you tell us how your Monday went?" Gareth asked.

Grace looked out the window and put her right hand to her forehead, tucking a stray strand behind her ear.

"Sure, I remember quite well. In the morning, I worked with Eleonor to process the loans. There were two large groups from Block B. It was intense, the girls were commenting on the last episode of *Night of the Vampire*. Hannah was disgruntled and raised her voice because two DVDs of the third and fourth series were not reserved for her last Friday. Strange, I thought, it was Eleonor on duty on Friday, and she never forgets to reserve materials for someone. But might be a bit distracted by her daughter's health problems."

"What happened then?" Gareth asked.

"Eleonor told me that Diane was working in the *Harper Room*, there were new books and DVDs to be processed."

"Did you see her?"

"Sure, I got there after the group from Block B left with the officer. I wanted to see what new series of films were brought. In fact, Eleonor sent me to get some DVDs from there," Grace said.

"Can you remember what time it was when you were there?"

"Sure, it was after 10:30, maybe 10:45."

"How was Diane, what was she doing?"

"She was processing DVDs, she looked okay to me. She asked me if Helen was coming to work that afternoon. I confirmed and said that Helen was considering applying for a new job with *Carlton Trust.*"

"What job?"

"*Listener*," answered Grace. "This job would help her advance and then apply for the *mentor* position."

"What did Diane answer?"

"She said that it was a good idea and then asked if Helen was happy with her job in the library."

"Did she seem interested?"

"Yes, she did," said Grace. "Diane was very open, she liked to chat with us and help us with various tips to keep our minds and bodies busy. *Girls liked her*," she said slightly confidentially.

"What happened next?" Carol asked after making a note in her notebook. Carol caught the idea that it was something very special for female prisoners to like a member of the prison staff.

"I didn't stay long, Eleanor called me, another group from another block was about to come and I had to be there to help her."

"How do you help her, exactly?" Gareth asked.

"My task is to look for the DVDs the residents want to borrow. The disks are held in the drawers behind the desk, not in the cases on the shelves as you might think. It is believed that they can be used as weapons. There are only empty DVD cases on the shelves. The girls choose which movies they want to see, take the cases from the shelves, and give them to Eleonor who puts the required discs inside."

"So, you retrieve the DVD discs, don't you?"

"Yes, you know, Eleonor doesn't have enough time to look for each one, especially when we have groups of 15 girls. Some of the girls are very demanding and noisy. We must work very quickly."

"I understand now. What else happened? Did you see if Diane left the room? Or did someone break into it?"

"I cannot remember. Maybe a few but I'm not sure."

"Can you make a little try?" Gareth said.

"Amanda, I suppose, at a certain point. She came out with a puzzle box. We keep puzzles there on a shelf. Karen then stayed for a few minutes. Eleonor went in there briefly to make sure Diane was there. She is very careful with this room."

"Was the door open?"

"Yes, it was open. Otherwise, the girls would not have entered. The residents from Block B are not very noisy and Diane held the door open for a while."

"Did Diane come out in the morning?"

"Of course not. Eleonor had asked her to hurry and finish processing two boxes of books and three DVDs. They were backlogged from last week. Diane didn't really enjoy doing this, but she had to finish by the end of the day."

"Did the door stay open all morning?"

Grace thought for a moment and her gaze became confused.

"I…I don't really know, I cannot remember," she murmured hesitantly.

Carol looked at her briefly and wondered what had upset the girl. Gareth notices and offers her a glass of water.

"If you feel tired, we can continue another time," he said.

"I'm fine, the girl smiled more relaxed, we can continue now."

"What happened then?"

"I worked with Eleonor for the group from Block C, then followed a third group of residents who came from the education department. It was quieter and more relaxed, only five-six from what I remember. We then went to lunch at 11:30 when it was *free movement*. It's time when we finish the program as well."

"Okay. Did you see Diane after that?"

"Not then. As I said, I had left for lunch at 11:30 am and I returned around 1:40 pm. She opened the door for me from the education department. I had come there with some of the residents who were attending math class. They remained there, I popped into the library."

"Why did you return to the library, it was Helen's shift, as far as I know?" Gareth asked.

"Yes, it's true, but Hannah had asked me to get her a book. As I forgot to take it in the morning, I had to pop in and take it after lunch. Diane opened the door for me from the education department and let me look for the book, it took a little while, about 15 minutes. Then came Kristin who let me go out. It was before free movement. We have free movement at 11:30, 2:30 and 4:30, when the inward gates are open and we can move between the blocks and the administrative buildings, including the library. I had to get to the gym."

"Did Diane hang out with you, then?"

"No, she did not. She was working on the computer in Eleonor's office."

"Was Eleonor there?"

"No, she was not. Diane said that Eleonor had left for a personal reason. Kristin was expected to serve at the desk in the afternoon."

"How was Diane like then?" Carol asked.

"She was as usual. She was checking her email I suppose and eating a sandwich. She didn't seem too excited because she still had a lot of work to do," she said.

Carol and Gareth thanked her for the very useful information. Grace smiled excitedly and told them she was willing to help anytime.

Helen Evans entered the *Carlton Room* a few minutes later.

She was short and stout, with short, boyish red hair, over which she wore a colourful Scottish cap. Helen had a firm look and his green eyes sparkled smartly. The dark circles and deep wrinkles under the eyes made Carol assume that she was approaching 50 years old and that life in prison was not easy for her to bear.

She sat down in the chair with a confident and casual air.

"I'm very sorry for Diane, I don't really have anything to say. Unfortunately, I didn't see her at all on Monday, I only worked with Kristin," she said.

Carol noticed a slight tremor in the woman's hands and her downright defensive attitude.

"Can you tell us about your schedule in the library on Monday?"

"Sure, I arrived at 2:30 p.m., Kristin was already here. She told me that Eleonor had had to leave at lunchtime and suggested that we must work together on processing the loans during the afternoon until 4:30 when the program ended. She also said that Diane was working in the *Harper Room* and had been instructed not to be disturbed. She was a little ironic, letting me know that she had no intention of communicating with Diane, they didn't really like each other. It was busy in the afternoon, we had three big crazy groups, but there were the officers with them. No trouble on Monday."

"Did you notice if the door to the *Harper Room* was open?"

"It was closed for sure," answered Helen.

"How can you be so sure?" Gareth asked.

"Because the residents in Block C are very noisy. Diane wanted to make sure she wasn't disturbed when she was working. She usually kept the door closed."

"Did you see if Diane came out or someone got in?"

Helen hesitated for a moment.

"I don't know for sure, I was behind the desk, it is not always visible from there. Then I was busy, I had to look for various books in the library. She could have gone out or someone could have entered. I'm not sure."

"What do you think about Diane, did you work well with her?" Carol asked.

"Yes, I did. She was a good colleague, empathetic, she was interested in life in prison."

"Interested in what sense?" Gareth wanted to know.

"She used to question the girls about various things, about the staff in the prison, for example, and she was very curious to know how the officers behaved with us."

"Why do you think she was doing this?"

"I don't know, she was probably curious," Helen said, shrugging her shoulders innocently.

"Any idea if Diane got along better with someone?" Carol asked.

"There was someone, but she died a few months ago, Deborah. They talked often and Deborah told us that Diane was special, very different from what she seemed. Intelligent and compassionate, she said."

"How did Deborah die?"

"A heart attack, poor Deborah had heart problems, they said. She had a life sentence, she was transferred from another prison, also in Yorkshire I guess," added Helen.

"Thank you, Helen, you have been a great help to us," said Carol.

The woman stood up from her chair with a dignified air and headed for the doorway.

Carol leaned back in her chair and leafed through her notebook saying:

"From what we have so far, on Monday, Diane returned to the library at 1:57 pm. She was last seen alive sometime after 2:00 pm when she opened the door for Grace from the education department. Grace is the last person to see Diane alive, as far as we know. Around 2:20, Kristin came, but she did not see Diane. It was Grace informing her that Diane was working in the *Harper Room*. According to these, we can get a first conclusion, that the murder might take place after 2:10, after Grace left. See. In the interval 2:10-2:20, it is unlikely, but not impossible, was too short and risky. The killer apparently knew the library staff's schedule and habits. After Kristin's arrival until her departure at 4:30 pm, it is again hard to believe that anyone would have risked sneaking into the *Harper Room* and being seen. The officers who escorted the resident groups, Kristin, or Helen, could come into the *Harper Room* at any time. We should consider the possibility that the killer slipped through the door of the IT room."

"It makes more sense to me that Diane was killed after 4:30 pm after Kristin and Helen left," Gareth said.

"It's a shame that Helen and Kristin don't recall if Diane left or if someone entered the *Harper Room* between 2:30 and 4:30 pm," Carol continued without hearing what Gareth had said. "Let's check with Eleonor Wilson what happened in the IT room on Monday."

Eleanor Wilson was in her office working on a computer. Carol greeted and asked her, "Can we check, please, if anyone was in the IT room on Monday after 2:00 pm?"

"There was no one in that room. George, the IT teacher, is on his annual leave this week," answered Eleonor calmly. "There are no IT courses this week, I'm sure."

"That room is locked if there are no classes, I assume?"

"Yes, it is locked indeed. But the door can be unlocked with the small key that the prison officers and staff have on their chains."

"So any member of the prison staff and officer can enter the IT room using the small key from the key chain? And from there, it needs that little key from your drawer to unlock the door to the *Harper Room*," Carol said.

"Exactly," Eleonor said. "Or it can be unlocked from the inside, of course."

"The murderer could come in from the IT room if Diane opened the door, am I right?" Gareth asked. "The murderer could get out anyway, the door locks automatically; there is no need to lock it back."

Eleanor Wilson nodded her head in approval.

"Could it be one of the prisoners?" Carol asked.

"It could be, but only if someone had unlocked the door to the IT room. As I said that door is locked if there are no classes there; residents don't have access there."

Lunchtime was approaching. Eleonor Wilson led them to the exit and asked what the chances were that the library would be open again in the coming days. Gareth replied that it was expected in a few days, he was still waiting for the coroner's final report.

Carol glanced hastily at her watch.

"Let's go eat, what do you think, *White Tiger*, today?" It was their favourite pub on the way to their headquarters in Bradford.

Gareth nodded gladly, and they got into the car together. Twenty minutes later, they were getting into the *White Tiger*.

Some Preliminary Conclusions

Gareth let Carol slip into the seat behind the table and flopped wearily into the chair in front of her. They had ordered at the bar, were both hungry and were eagerly waiting.

"Complicated story, do you think so?" Gareth said with his eyes on the bar.

"Yes, what strikes me is that Diane appears in two completely different versions. Some witnesses say she was a toxic, selfish, uncompassionate person with a dark past. Others speak of an intelligent, empathetic, helpful Diane. What the truth could be? I think we should figure out more about her past, my instinct tells me that something from her past can help us with the investigation. And it may be connected to the investigation she was doing. Unfortunately, we don't have her laptop, which could give us a clue."

"Could help us indeed," Gareth said in disbelief. "She has discovered a corruption case in the prison, perhaps. Could be something connected to her uncle's death, Brian Dunmore, last year. She was talking to the prisoners, who of course had some information. But I'd rather think Patterson is involved. He had every reason, Diane wanted a divorce; he was going to be left with nothing. The idea of killing her in prison was perfect, it's the right place; one of the prisoners could be charged with murder."

"I find it hard to believe that a prisoner could do this, at least without one of the staff member's involvement. But we should not rule out this possibility. I'm thinking about the story with the keys. Why did Diane have keys for officers and how had she managed to get them, where had she got the password? From her husband maybe? And most of all, why did Diane need access to the prisoners' cells? How can we find this out? Should we talk to someone close to Deborah, the prisoner that Diane used to talk to more? I have a feeling that Helen knows more than she lets us know."

"Maybe the murderer replaced the keys. He put his keys in the holder and took hers to make sure there wouldn't be an alarm."

"That leads us to your favourite hypothesis that Patterson would have committed the murder," said Carol with an ironic smile. "Based on your reasoning, the murderer would have had to know the password to the staff cabinet to return the set of keys taken from Diane, am I correct? Do you think the murderer asked her for the password before killing her?"

"Huh," said Gareth resignedly, "but we cannot completely exclude this scenario. Maybe Diane told him in a different context. I think it makes sense. Anyway, I agree that we should dig into Diana's past a bit, which means a visit to the Dunmore family. That won't be easy," Gareth said. "But here comes the food, let's feed the grey cells a little," Gareth said with twinkling eyes at the waitress approaching with what appeared to be their food.

A Little Journey into Diane's Past

The next day, Carol had managed to arrange a meeting at 11:00 am with Daniel Dunmore, Diane's father, and was hurrying to get to *Stratford Street*, where her parents live.

She parked the car in front of an old two-level red brick building. *A rather modest house for a wealthy family*, Carol thought. She stepped down the groomed driveway to the main entrance of the house and cautiously pressed the doorbell button. A tall, brunette young woman exquisitely dressed in a dark office suit, who introduced herself as the Dunmore family's chief assistant, promptly opened the door. The young woman invited her to a downstairs salon and asked her to wait a few minutes because Daniel Dunmore had an unexpected phone call. She suggested Carol help herself with a cup of tea or coffee from a small brown table in the middle of the little salon. Carol thanked the chief assistant before she disappeared behind the door with the same discreet smile with which she had greeted her.

Carol sat comfortably in the armchair and sipped her coffee scanning discreetly the little salon. She realised, suddenly, that she was not alone. On a couch near the window sat an elderly woman, dressed in a black dress, contrasting sharply with her military-cropped, bright red dyed hair. A huge necklace of grass-coloured beads covered her plunging and daring cleavage. The woman was looking at a huge black album but after Carol's arrival, she put it on her lap and stared at her.

"Are you from the police?" The old woman asked.

Carol put the cup on the plate and nodded quietly.

"I presume you came to ask us about Diane," she said disapprovingly. "This girl has caused us nothing but trouble," she said taking off her black glasses, which she placed carefully on the couch near her. A pair of blue, ophthalmic eyes looked at her with obvious curiosity. "And look how she ended, the old woman said, as if to bring us nothing but annoyance."

"Do you live here?" Carol asked politely.

"Of course, I live here, I'm Kathryn, Daniel Dunmore's sister," said the woman annoyed that someone could dare not recognise her. "Who knows who else she messed with?" The woman said with a sigh. "I always told them that this girl was not going to end well," she then said with satisfaction in her voice.

Kathryn Dunmore stood up and poured herself a cup of tea, her hands shaking.

"Like father like son, I told them not to take her, but they didn't listen to me," said the old woman with satisfaction. "How can you leave the family fortune in the hands of someone like her?"

"What do you mean?" Carol asked trying to keep a restrained voice.

Kathryn Dunmore seemed not to listen and put the empty cup back on the table. She then took the album back and looked carefully at one of the photos.

"Look here," she said, looking at a little photograph, "Diane was here with Elise, a lovely creature. Diane was a little nasty girl, running around and making trouble." Carol came closer and looked at the photo the old woman pointed to. A little blonde girl with a sad smile and a bit mature for her age. Next to her was a young woman in her 20s, with her hair tied back, wearing a long dress.

"Who is Elise, do you know her?" Carol asked.

"Sure, I do, I have an elephant memory. She was Diane's governess, they got along very well."

"Where is she now, do you have any idea?" Carol questioned again. She slowly took out the old photo and looked at the back of it. A hand in school writing had written the year, 1950, and added briefly: *With my dear friend, Elise.*

"She left, a long time ago, she must be in Glenshire now with her family," said Kathryn Dunmore.

The young assistant opened the door quietly and said in a neutral voice, "Mr Daniel Dunmore is waiting for you, come with me, please."

Carol stood up and headed for the door. Kathryn Dunmore seemed not to notice her departure looking into the family album.

They walked down a long corridor and then stepped into a large and bright room that seemed to be the assistant's desk. She pointed to a side door that led to Daniel Dunmore's office.

Diane's father greets her with a sad smile. He was a tall man with greying hair slicked back. The light blue eyes were expressive and agile. He shook her hand, and she felt the firmness. The man invited her to take a seat with a natural gesture.

"Please excuse my wife, she is not feeling well, unfortunately." Then he added, "Terrible news, our little poor Diane.

I told her not to work there, it was a dangerous environment, but she didn't listen. She had a strong personality, she always only did what she wanted," Dunmore said.

"Can you tell me when you last saw her?" Carol asked.

"We saw each other very rarely, especially after marrying Chris Patterson. I think it was about two weeks ago when she came here on a Saturday. She said that she wanted a divorce, and I remember I told her that she had finally made the right decision."

"Did she seem changed to you? I mean, like someone who wants to change her life. Their marriage had not run well for the last year, I understood."

"She didn't seem changed, I just suggested she talk to the family lawyer. And then she had to expect a war with Patterson who did not give up his fortune easily."

"Do you see Chris Patterson able to commit a murder?"

"Yes, I really do. I think he is capable of it. He is an unscrupulous young man. From the moment he met my daughter, he knew what he wanted. I told Diane, but she didn't bother to listen to me, she only always did what she thought was best for her."

Carol politely nodded, then recounted her conversation with Kathryn Dunmore in the living room.

"Can you tell me, please, what your sister meant?"

Daniel Dunmore threw his head back with a confused look and then said looking down at the floor "Diane is, she was adopted. She was a month old when we took her from an adoption home. We could not have children and I made this decision together with Marian, my wife, to adopt a child. I would kindly ask you to be discreet with these details, I doubt that it can help the investigation."

Carol assured him of her discretion, and Dunmore continued, "Diane was a rebellious child, we couldn't control her; she had a strong personality. I told her she was adopted. She knew it. She was not interested in the family company. She said she still did not know what she wanted to do in life, but she wanted to be free. She decided to go to university and study journalism, I supported her financially, but she got bored quickly. After two years, she gave up. She returned to Sheffield but did not know where to get a job. I found her a position at a local newspaper, but she didn't stay there for more than five months. She got bored. She had a special talent for finding herself in the middle of local scandals."

"Did Diane have a will?"

"No, she never thought of doing it, she was too young, 27 years old. At this age, you think you are immortal. Patterson will inherit the house and her share of the stock in the company. Hard times for us," he said worriedly.

Dunmore glanced briefly and meaningly at his watch, and Carol understood that they were nearing the end of the discussion.

"Do you have any idea what enemies Diane had, who could wish her death?" She asked.

"Diane was a very sociable and friendly person, I find it hard to believe that she had enemies. I would carefully investigate Patterson. I understand he was in debt. Anyway, I look forward to you keeping me updated on the progress of the investigation. I don't know anyone else, but if I remember, I'll let you know. You may call me any time."

Carol assured him that they would do so and said goodbye.

"One more question, please. I understood that Diane was very close to her nanny, Elise, do you know where she might be now?"

Daniel Dunmore put his hand to his forehead and tried to remember.

"Oh, that was a long time ago, I don't even remember. Please speak to Hannah, our secretary. She might have the address, just in case. She is a very meticulous and organised person."

Carol thanked Daniel Dunmore once more and headed for the doorway. Hannah easily found Elisa Brown's address on the computer and gave her contact details. Elise's last known address was in Glenshire, a few miles from Bradford. Carol decided to pay her a visit. She asked Hanna's consent to make a phone call to Elise Brown and make sure the address was still available. It was her lucky day, Carol thought, the address was right, Elise Brown was at home looking forward to having a chat about Diane Dunmore.

The detective arrived in Glenshire 30 minutes later and went into the first pub for lunch. It seemed like a quiet little town, and the bartender easily gave her advice on how to get to Elise Brown's house.

"Lissy is at home, for sure. Since her husband died, her health has not been going well. The girls have both gone to London and she only has a younger sister here, whom she visits daily."

After a frugal lunch and a refreshing coffee, Carol felt ready for a new adventure. Elise Brown lived in a small studio on the ground floor of a well-kept house located on a street parallel to the main street of the town.

Elise Brown appeared to be in her mid-50s, a cheerful and bubbly woman. When she heard of Diane's death, her face got pale and she made a visible effort to keep her tears.

"Oh, my poor little girl, what a sad destiny, she couldn't escape her own fate."

"I understand that she was an adopted child, but she didn't manage to adapt to the Dunmore family," said Carol.

"Yes, she didn't have parental warmth, poor thing. The Dunmores were not suited to her temperament," said the woman, wiping her eyes with a crumpled handkerchief, which she put back in her pocket.

"Was it known who the real parents were?" Carol asked.

Elise looked at Carol in surprise; then said furtively, "I thought you knew. Diane was Brian Dunmore's child, Daniel Dunmore's young brother. A good man, but a weak character. He was suffering from heavy depression, and there were rumours that he was taking drugs. By the way, he died about a year ago, I read in the newspapers. Brian met Diane's mother when she was a prisoner in Sheffield Prison. He was an officer there. A very sad story. Her mum died a few months after giving birth to Diane. Brian Dunmore was very affected since then he started having health problems, he drank a lot, I understand. I know the whole story from Diane, her parents told her when she turned 18. We kept in touch after I left Stratford, she said, Diane called me from time to time."

"How was she getting along with her natural father, Brian Dunmore?" Carol asked.

"In a way, well, he was the only one who had influence over her; Diane was a difficult person. Brian intervened many times to get her out of trouble with the police. I think he felt guilty for not taking on her upbringing. The Dunmore family had decided then that it was not advisable to be involved in a scandal. Brian was an officer at Sheffield Prison and officers were not allowed to have relations with female prisoners. The Dunmores wanted to avoid any scandal that could affect their business. They decided to adopt the girl. Brian has never married since Diane's mother's death and lived quite a secluded life suffering from depression. He stayed with us for a while, at Dunmore residence, then he moved out and lived alone."

"It's a shame we can't figure out more details about Brian Dunmore's working time at Sheffield Prison. Not from his family anyway. They want to keep quiet on this old story. Do you know if Brian Dunmore had any friends or anyone close to him?"

"Yes, I remember a former colleague from Sheffield visiting him several times, he must be retired now, but I can't remember his name. The Dunmores can also tell you his name; they must have invited him to the funeral a year ago."

Carol took careful notes and realised with not too much pleasure that she would have to call the Dunmores again.

"You helped us a lot," said Carol gladly. She gave Elise a business card saying to call her anytime if she remembered any details that might help the investigation into Diane's death. After all, the governess was probably the only one who had loved her and truly regretted Diane's death, Carol thought.

It was nearly 5:00 pm when she was driving back to Brandford and texted Gareth to meet her at Bradford HQ.

Gareth was waiting for her feverishly, with two cups of tea ready.

"How was the meeting with Dunmore?" He asked curiously.

Carol recounted her discussion with Daniel Dunmore then about the road to Glenshire and the information she received from Elise Brown.

"Very interesting," Gareth said excitedly. "That would explain Diane's behaviour. Sheffield Prison, you say? Quite bizarre, Deborah Hall was there before she was transferred to Clayton."

Carol sipped from her teacup and encouraged him to continue.

"I don't have as much information as you," Gareth said with apparent modesty. "I had a talk with Helen about Deborah Hall. Deborah reportedly spent over 20 years in Sheffield Prison before being transferred to Clayton. She was a very quiet prisoner. She barely spoke to someone. It was what caught Helen's attention that Diane was able to get close to Deborah and made her talk a bit more. Helen said she caught Diane and Deborah talking behind the bookcase, and they seemed to change the subject when they saw her approaching. Deborah was suffering from a heart issue. She had already had a heart attack in Sheffield Prison. And the second one was deadly. She was found dead in her room in August this year, and the cause was, without any doubt, a heart attack. Diane was visibly affected by her death."

"What could she have said to Diane?"

"Helen did not seem to know, but she thought Diane was very attached to Deborah. I looked into Deborah's file. Life sentence. Transferred to Clayton Prison from Sheffield on 17 July to a closed but more relaxed regime, in Block B, because she had behaved appropriately. Deborah had a friend in Sheffield Prison, Carrie Armstrong, I checked and she was still there. Listening to your findings about Dunmore, I'm inclined to believe that Deborah told Diane something about Brian Dunmore's relationship with her mother. By the way, Diane was there two weeks ago," Helen said.

"How did Helen know about it?"

"Diane told her," said Gareth

"Maybe we should go there, what do you think?"

"Sure, I'll call to set up a meeting for tomorrow," Gareth said. "Now, let me tell you what information comes out of the report."

"Well, what does it say?"

"The coroner's final report says that a blonde thread that did not belong to Diane was found on her brown jacket. It comes from a wig for sure."

"This is interesting. Why would Diane have worn a blonde wig? It was her jacket, wasn't it?"

"Sure. Kristin confirmed that it was the jacket that Diane used to wear every day. Then, the report says the death occurred between noon and 5 pm. Diane hadn't eaten her lunch anyway. There were no signs of poisoning, the murder weapon appeared to be a rectangular metal object, and death occurred because of repeated blows. Nothing was found in the room that could be considered the murder weapon."

"Hang on. Did you say that she hadn't had her lunch? Grace told us Diane was eating a sandwich when she saw her shortly after 2:00 pm. Odd, I'll see my notes again. Now, I'm going to check my email," Carol said thoughtfully.

"I also spoke with the duty officer from the education department. He said he had checked out of the library on Monday after 6:00 pm as he usually does. He does this every evening after the staff members have left to make sure no prisoners are left there. Everything seemed to be fine in every room in the library and the door to the IT room was locked as usual. He didn't unlock the little storage room to check inside, it's not part of officer protocol to do that."

"Good to know this," Carol said thoughtfully. "Do you want to speak in Sheffield Prison?"

Half an hour later, Gareth said triumphantly,

"Tomorrow we are going to Sheffield Prison, I spoke to the manager," said Gareth with a self-confident smile. "I couldn't find a recent photo of Diane, unfortunately, Eleonor Wilson didn't come to the library today. But Kristin gave me a photo of Eleonor and Diane from last year at a library event. I think it might help us at the meeting with Carrie Armstrong."

"Good idea, Gareth," said Carol, focused on reading a message in her email. "We should go home now, it's almost seven o'clock," she said, realising that she was feeling very tired. *We'll have plenty of time tomorrow*, she thought and switched the computer off.

Visiting Sheffield Prison

The police car was running cautiously on the M1 towards Sheffield. It was almost 9:30 am and the drive to Sheffield shouldn't last more than an hour and 30 minutes. The prison was on *Attercliff Hill*, a street perpendicular to the highway, close to the town entrance.

It was raining lightly, but both detectives were observing the gorgeous Autumnal brown colours of the trees on both sides of the road.

"Last night I checked my notes from Grace Davies's statement. I was right, she told us that Diane was eating a sandwich when she opened the door for her shortly after 2:00 pm. But the coroner's report shows that Diane had nothing in her stomach. And we found a sandwich in the car parked in front of the prison. I think we should check again with Grace."

"Maybe she was confused, you know these things happen," Gareth said smoothly.

"Maybe indeed," Carol replied.

They arrived on time and easily spotted a parking space outside Sheffield Prison. The building was smaller and less depressing than Clayton. Michael Smith, the manager of the prison, greeted them with a friendly smile and led them into one of the visiting rooms where they were to speak with Carrie Armstrong.

"An officer will bring Carrie in a few minutes, I hope she can help you with the investigation," he said friendly. "If you need access to her file, let me know; I'll talk to the administrative department."

Carol and Gareth thanked him for the assistance and settled comfortably around a little table packed with lots of pamphlets and children's books. The visiting room was not very large, a few paintings of Disney characters gave it a warm and familiar appearance. Several cupboards were full of toys, colouring books, footballs, and DVDs. A large TV screen on one of the walls. Three round tables with folding chairs in very bright colours.

Carrie Armstrong was small with long greying hair topped with a green frog beanie. The blue eyes were smart, with a lively and direct gaze. The face was surprisingly long and dry, with a sharp chin, and strong, firm jaws. She greeted them cheerfully and settled comfortably into one of the chairs in front of them. She did not seem to be embarrassed by the lack of front teeth, an obvious sign that the woman had a problem related to drug addiction.

"Cold weather these days, isn't it? I think Cornwall is also cold for November. Times have changed a lot, the climate, we're heading for extreme temperatures," Carrie said.

Carol agreed with a smile.

"You're from Cornwall, aren't you?" She asked.

Carrie nodded with a dignified look.

"My daughter lives there with her husband and three children. It's not easy for them to come here and visit me, it's quite far," she said with a hint of regret in his voice.

Gareth raised his voice and asked in a friendly way, "Do you know Deborah Hall? She was here for a while."

"Of course, I know Debbie, she was my friend, I was very sad that she left, but we used to talk on the phone from time to time. She had been suffering for the last two years from heart issues; she had a weak heart."

"How was she like?"

"She was a quiet woman, she didn't talk to anyone around here, but with me she was different. She used to say she wouldn't last long, my dear Debbie…"

"Has anyone recently come to visit you to ask about Deborah?"

Carrie answered promptly, "Indeed, there was a woman, Diane, about two weeks ago, I think. She said she knew Debbie from Clayton Prison where she had recently been transferred. Diane spoke very nicely about poor Debbie, I thought she knew Debbie quite well. But why do you want to know about this?"

"Why did she come to visit you, did you know that Debbie died?" Gareth said ignoring Carrie's question.

"Yes, I knew, my poor Debbie, she was aware her end was around. This woman, Diane, wanted to know more about an old story that Debbie had told her. Diane said she would like to write a book about her story."

"What story?"

"As I was saying, it was an old story, over 20 years old, about a girl, Iris, who had a relationship with an officer from the prison here and got pregnant. Relationships between prisoners and prison staff are not allowed. Deborah said this girl, Iris, was very beautiful. Iris had killed her husband in a fit of jealousy, she was emotionally unstable; she had received a life sentence. The relationship with the officer had been very discreet, no one had known about it. Besides, this had been happening for more than 25 years, as I mentioned. Debbie said this girl died shortly after giving birth to a baby girl. She is said to have committed suicide, but there were rumours that she was murdered. They gave the girl up for adoption and the officer had to go, I don't know if he was punished but I doubt it. I didn't know Iris, I wasn't here then, but I know the story from Debbie. She used to say that it was a very sad story at the time."

"Did you tell Diane about that?"

"Yes, I did but she already knew about this story. She wanted to know if I had further details. Deborah was Iris's close friend. Diane said that she wanted to reveal the truth about Iris and that her book might cause some trouble. She also said something about her manager, that she apparently worked in Sheffield Prison at that time being involved in the investigation. She wanted to know if I met that woman, but I've been here for five years only so I could not meet her."

"Her manager? Do you mean Eleanor Wilson?"

"Cannot remember the name precisely. Diane told me that Debbie recognised her from Sheffield Prison where she had worked in the library many years ago."

"Could you please have a look at this picture?" Gareth said, handing her the photo of Diane and Eleonor.

"Ah," Carrie said, "I remember this picture, Diane showed it to me. I couldn't help her, unfortunately, as I said, I've been in Sheffield for five years."

Carol and Gareth looked at each other in silence.

"You said you kept in touch with Deborah after she was transferred to Clayton Prison. Did she tell you anything else about this story, did she refer to it since she was in Clayton?"

"No, she did not. She called me a few times, but we only talked about families, and she complained that her joints hurt more and more. She said she had a bigger puzzle collection in Clayton, it was her passion, did you know?"

Carol thanked Carrie and suggested letting them know if she remembered anything else. Gareth went to find the officer who was to lead her back to her block.

After Carrie Armstrong left the room, Carol and Gareth made their way to the manager's office.

"Well, have you found out what you wanted to know?" Michael Smith asked them jovially.

"Actually, we have. Very helpful indeed," Carol said. "Do you think we could figure out if a certain person worked here 20 or so years ago?"

"Of course," he said. "I wasn't here," he said with a big smile, "but I'm going to talk to the archives, to help us. What is that person's name?"

"Eleonor Wilson," Carol said.

"Denise, will you put me through to the archives department, please?" Smith addressed the secretary on the phone.

An hour later, Carol and Gareth were in the car on their way to Bradford.

They found out some interesting information in Sheffield Prison. Brian Dunmore, Diane's natural father, had worked in Sheffield during the time Iris Clark had been imprisoned there. Apparently, Iris Clark was Diane's natural mother. According to the inquest report, Iris had committed suicide during a deep depression crisis. Death was caused by a significant dose of anti-depressants. The investigation did not reveal who might have supplied her with the anti-depressants. Dunmore was considered morally guilty, but the investigation was not completed, someone stepped in, and the case was closed. Eleonor Wilson was then working as a librarian and appeared as a witness at the inquest.

"Maybe Eleonor Wilson should have mentioned this episode from her life, don't you think?" Carol said.

"Yes, I do. We must have another discussion with her as soon as possible," said Gareth. "Maybe she didn't think it was important."

It was almost 3:00 pm when they arrived at the headquarters. Carol learnt that they had been called by Kristin Burton that morning. The woman wanted to talk to them about the investigation into Diane's death. Carol dialled the phone number for the Clayton Prison library. It was Kristin Burton who answered saying that Eleonor Wilson was not at work as she had taken two days off and would be back at work the next day. Carol asked if it was possible to talk to Grace, and Kristin assured her that she'd talk to the duty officer to set up a meeting.

"Let's go shortly to Clayton," Carol said.

The prison library was very noisy when they got there. Kristin Burton was behind the desk with Helen with red exhausted faces. A group of around 15 female prisoners stood outside the desk holding books and DVDs and waiting to be processed for a loan. The girls were laughing and talking loudly when Carol and Gareth entered the library. Carol sat down in a chair and motioned for Kristin to take her time; they could wait.

After the group of prisoners left the library, Kristin invited them into the *Harper Room*.

"You wanted to talk. Did you recall any details?" Gareth asked impatiently.

"Yes, I did. I wanted to talk to you about what Chris once told me about Diane. He believed that Diane was doing a personal investigation and had discovered a case of corruption in the administration of a prison, but he didn't tell me which one. Diane wanted to write a book about it."

"He didn't give you any other details, did he?"

"No, he did not but I have the feeling that he knows more, maybe he saw something or learnt from Diane; he didn't tell me."

"Maybe we should talk to Chris Patterson about this?" Gareth said

"Please don't tell him that you talked to me about this," Kristin said with fear in her voice.

"Do not worry, we have our suspicions too," Gareth answered

"He's working today, but you can call him tomorrow," Kristin added and headed to the main room to answer a phone that was ringing persistently.

Kristin returned after a few minutes to tell them that Grace was coming to the library to talk to them.

"I must leave now, I'm waiting for a group of residents, and I must be at the computer."

Gareth thanked her and after the woman left the room, he said to Carol, "Interesting that she remembered right now. She didn't tell us what prison it was. She knew something but not enough."

"She wants to save Patterson, that's for sure. She thought we suspected him, especially after the latest information about Diane's inheritance," Carol replied.

There was a short knock on the door and Grace entered with hesitant steps. "Good evening, I understand that you want to talk," she said shyly

"Yes, actually we wanted to check a small detail with you," said Carol. "You remember telling us that on the day she was murdered, Diane was having lunch when she unlocked the library door for you, she had a sandwich. You had come to pick up a book for Hannah before going to the gym."

"Yes, that's right, I remember," said the girl looking carefully at Carol.

"However, the coroner's report shows that Diane had not eaten anything that day."

"I might have been wrong," answered Grace with uncertainty in her voice, "it was a busy day then."

"Yes, it is possible," said Carol, "sometimes memory can play tricks on us."

Grace got up from her chair and walked over to the window. Her face had turned red, and her frightened gaze was fixed on the floor. It was a different Grace now, the shyness gone, she was like a small, hunted animal, in the position of self-defence.

"Am I a suspect? I didn't kill anyone. I don't remember anything since then," she said in a harsh voice.

Gareth stood up and tried to calm her down.

"Grace, calm down, no one is accusing you of anything."

"They're looking for a scapegoat, they want you to accuse me of a crime I didn't commit. What reason could I have to kill Diane? Unbelievable…unbelievable…unbelievable. I must talk to Eleonor; I must talk to her…"

"Calm down Grace, Carol also said. Nobody blamed you. Who are they, who are you referring to?"

Grace didn't say anything keeping her gaze fixed on the floor.

"Do you want me to get you a glass of water?" Gareth said with compassion.

The girl's face was getting redder, and her eyes were full of tears.

"Unbelievable…" she repeated absently, with a fixed gaze, as if trying to remember something.

The door suddenly opened, and Helen burst into the room.

"What did you tell her?" She said reproachfully. "Grace is very fragile." She put her arms around the girl's shoulders and tried to calm her down.

Helen pulled Grace towards the door and said, "We need to go to the medical service now. Grace needs a sedative. She meant Chris and Kristin, they had every reason to make Diane disappear and find a scapegoat in one of the prisoners," Helen added pointedly, then left the room with Grace.

Carol looked at Gareth puzzled.

"Grace said she had to talk to Eleonor, what did that mean? A bit odd. We'll have to have another chat with Eleonor Wilson when she gets back to the office."

"Until then, I would suggest we meet with Chris Patterson and see what he can tell us about this story with Diane's natural parents."

A New Discussion with Chris Patterson

Chris Patterson looked better than the last time they met. He had a lively look and seemed more relaxed. He invited them to take a seat in the living room offering them a drink.

"Well, did you make progress with the investigation?" He asked with a cheeky smile and sat comfortably in one of the armchairs.

"Yes, we did. There is some news compared to our last meeting. But nothing about an alleged case of prison corruption," Gareth said with a wry smile.

Patterson looked directly at him but did not reply.

"Do you know what Diane was chasing about her family?" Carol asked.

"Aha, so you found out that Diane was adopted. Strange family, huh?"

"Had she ever mentioned to you about her real parents?"

Chris Patterson blinked slightly, probably wondering just how much the two detectives knew.

"Diane was fascinated to learn the truth about her birth parents, especially her mother. She had apparently died in prison shortly after Diana was born under suspicious circumstances, she said. That's why Diane had started an investigation on her own and I think she had managed to pick up a trace, but she went too far maybe…" Chris said looking sadly further in front of him.

"What did she find out about her mother?" Carol asked.

"Her name was Iris and she was a fascinating woman, said Diane. She had killed her husband in a moment of jealousy and received a life sentence. She was a beautiful woman, but emotionally unstable and completely immature. She used to paint beautifully, she was very talented, Diane said. In fact, that's how she learnt about this story, from a fellow inmate of her mother's, to whom she had left some of her sketches."

"Was Deborah Hall that inmate?" Gareth asked.

"I don't recall exactly. A few weeks ago, Diane came home very excited, saying she was about to figure out important things about her real mother. You know, Brian, her uncle, meaning her real father, never wanted to talk about Iris. He apparently never fully recovered from her suicide. Diane said Brian held himself morally responsible for her mother's death and for not assuming the relationship with Iris."

"In what sense did he not assume?"

"He denied the relationship with Iris, under his family pressure. It seems that after Iris got pregnant, rumours about their relationship started circulating in the prison. Inquiries were made, he denied having an affair. Eventually, he was disciplinary moved, investigations stopped, his family is said to have stepped in and pushed for the case to be closed. On the other hand, Diane was saying that her mother hadn't exactly been a churchgoer, and Brian was beginning to have doubts that the little girl was his baby. The family encouraged his doubts. After Iris committed suicide, Brian realised that he had made a big mistake, that he had misjudged her, but it was too late. Since then, he has not recovered from this trauma."

"What did Diane think about it?"

"Diane thought that Iris had had a relationship in prison, it was true..."

"Was it possible that Brian Dunmore wasn't really her father?" Carol asked.

"She said that it was not necessarily with a man..."

"You mean Iris had a relationship with a woman? With whom?"

"Diane didn't keep me up to date with her research. She was just saying that she was going to publish a book that was going to cause a scandal in the former Sheffield Prison administration."

"Where did she get all the information?"

"It seems that from that prisoner, Deborah Hall. She had been at Sheffield Prison and arrived early this year in Clayton. She had met Iris Clark, they had been getting along together. She died a few months ago, I think. Deborah, yes, I remember now. Diane had seen some sketches of her and admired them, apparently her mother, Iris, had been very talented. Deborah then told her the story of Iris and Diane immediately saw the connection to Brian Dunmore and understood that they were her real parents. Life is so strange, isn't it? After all these years, to find out these terrible things by chance...Diane was very excited. Shortly after, Deborah died suddenly, but I understand she had serious heart problems."

"Did Diane talk to anyone about this story, anyone in the family?"

"I don't think so, she didn't get along with them. She told me because, in a way, she needed someone to listen to her and wanted to know my opinion."

"Or she needed you," said Gareth insinuatingly. "For example, how could she have access to keys that were only for officers?"

Chris Patterson avoided Gareth's gaze and gently cuddled the dog's crest.

"I don't know, Diane could be very inventive when she wanted to get something. Remember, she was an investigative journalist for a while."

"But why do you think she needed those keys? You can only make assumptions…" said Carol submissively.

"She might want to talk to the residents," Chris said. "It's incredible how much you can learn from them about prison life or prison staff. Diane knew how to get information from them, she also did them small commissions or offered them small gifts, chocolates and cigarettes."

Carol recalled that they had found several boxes of chocolates in Diane's car.

There was a persistent sound of a mobile phone in the next room. Chris stood up and left the room to answer. He came back a few minutes later and told them he had to leave for work.

"I hope I was of use to you," he said with a relaxed smile.

"Sure, very much," answered Gareth. "Stay in touch; let us know if you remember anything useful."

Carol and Gareth walked in silence to the car parked in front of the house.

“This guy is not as wicked as we imagined,” said Carol. “He knows more than he’s telling us for sure. There is someone else who knew about Diane’s research. What a shame Brian Dunmore is no longer alive! We should figure out more about his years in Sheffield. It’s time to have a discussion with his former colleague from Sheffield Prison. Can you call the Dunmores and get his address?”

“I would say that you have more chances to find out, Carol,” Gareth said smiling.

Another Short Journey into Diane's Past

Friday had started well. Carol had managed to have a brief conversation with Daniel Dunmore who discreetly asked if there was any progress in the investigation into his daughter's death. He vaguely remembered his brother's former friend, but expectedly suggested she ask Hannah, his efficient assistant, for details.

"Sure," Hannah said after a short pause, "Steven Morton was invited to Brian Dunmore's funeral last year." She gave Carol his address in Sheffield in Loxley and a telephone number. "He attended the funeral," Hannah said, "the phone number is quite recent and should be available."

Carol and Gareth found Steven Morton in Loxley, in a small but well-maintained flat where he lived with one of his sons. He was a tall, wiry fellow with a friendly look under bushy eyebrows and a high forehead. Glad to have guests, the man invited them to take a seat and offered them hot tea.

"Interesting, that you ask me about Brian," he said, "I'm sorry to hear from his girl that she died. She was a smart girl, I remember, but yes, she was a bit of a troublemaker, as well. I saw her at Brian's funeral, she looked like his mother; she had that seductive look of hers."

"So, you met Iris Clark, Diana's real mother?" Gareth asked.

"Yes, I did. She was a beautiful woman who twisted poor Brian's mind. He suffered a lot; he loved her. She loved him too, I think, but she was mentally and emotionally unstable."

"Did you know about their relationship?"

"Yes, I did. Brian had told me we were close. He said his family would never accept Iris. He was very unhappy, he said, a relationship with no future, but deep inside, he was hoping for a miracle to happen. Then she found out she was going to have a baby and she told him. I recall he was extremely happy. They were two dreamers; they didn't even think that a big scandal would follow. Then someone spread the rumour that Iris was having other relationships. Poor Brian got mad; he couldn't believe she could cheat on him."

"But how did this rumour start?" Carol asked.

"I don't know where it started, in prison the girls were talking, laughing. Poor Iris had to face all that gossip and evil."

"Do you remember what other relationships it would have been about?"

" No names were given, but it was rumoured that Iris had been with other officers. But I remember the girls talking about Iris having a relationship with a woman."

"This is strange, with whom, was it known then?"

"A woman who worked at the library, I don't remember her name. She was also a witness at the death inquest. Because Iris spent a lot of time in the library, the girls said that Iris and that girl were more than friends, but who knows? It remained a mystery. I tend to believe it was true, Iris was fragile, life in prison is not easy; she needed someone to support her. After

Brian left especially. I remember once that I caught her sitting with the librarian behind a book stand, holding hands tenderly, as lovers do. There was something between them. But I didn't tell Brian, I didn't want to make him suffer more."

"We read in the archives about how Iris died, but what do you think about her suicide?"

"I don't know further. She was found dead in her cell after an overdose of painkillers. It is not known how she got those tablets and who gave them to her. She suffered from chronic depression. I remember. The conclusion was that she would have stolen the tablets from the medical centre. The case was closed; the Dunmore family pressed for it. Brian was already transferred, and the local mass media was against him. Daniel Dunmore adopted the little girl soon after, and there was silence in the case of poor Iris."

"How about the librarian?"

"She testified then. But she got some days off after Iris's death. I didn't see her at the library, then she got a job in another library, I understood."

"Had you met Diane recently?"

"A few weeks ago, she was at my place to talk about Iris Clark. I told her what I told you. She asked me about the girl in the library and she showed me a photo of her. She seemed to be the same, but maybe my memory is wrong. It was an old story from over 25 years ago."

"Why did Diane want to know about the girl in the library?"

"Well, she said they worked together at Clayton, she was her manager at the library."

"Yes," said Carol thoughtfully. "What a coincidence to work with someone who knew her mother? Did she look excited?"

"She was just very anxious to know about the circumstances in which her mother died. I asked her why she was trying to bring up the past. She didn't believe her mother killed herself. I told her that she was wrong, little Iris had the perfect suicidal profile; she was mentally weak and depressed. It is enough to just look at her sketches and you can see what a dark mind and lonely spirit little Iris was."

The two detectives have to admit that the investigation was finally leading to a certain track.

A New Discussion with Eleonor Wilson

They found Eleanor Wilson working alone in front of the computer. She looked more tired, with red lids and deep dark circles.

"I had to take a few days off to spend with my daughter, she is not feeling well."

"I understand, I hope she will be better soon. Maybe you should seek professional help," Carol said sympathetically.

"November is a difficult month for her, the depression is stronger this part of the year. November and January," she said thoughtfully, "are difficult and challenging months for my family."

"We're sorry to hear that. Can we talk a little bit about the Diane Dunmore case, please?"

"Sure. The first residents arrive at 9:30 am. I wanted to ask you how the investigation is going, I hope you complete it quickly."

"Yes, we are making some progress. Can you tell us why you didn't mention that you met Diane's real mother?"

Eleanor Wilson stopped and looked at them in dismay.

"Oh, I didn't think it might be relevant to the investigation."

"Any detail might be. So, did Diane tell you about her real mother?" Carol asked.

"Yes, she told me at one point. It's been a long time, anyway," Eleonor said and got up from her chair to open a drawer in an adjacent cabinet. "I don't see how that matters to her inquiry," she said in surprise.

"As my colleague said, any detail can be important," said Gareth

"Do you think this old story could be related to her death?"

"Diane was doing her own investigation related to a corruption case in the prison where you worked at the time, in Sheffield."

"Oh, I thought that investigation was completed. What could she find out that could threaten her life, though?" Eleanor asked.

"I don't know, maybe something related to the suicide of her mother, Iris Clark. Maybe it wasn't suicide. What was she like, did you know her well?"

Eleanor Wilson looked down at the floor with a sad air.

"Iris committed suicide, that's for sure. She was a special girl, but totally reckless. She fell in love with a man who didn't deserve her. She was extremely talented. I think her paintings are still in the library in Sheffield. Her suicide was a real drama, a real drama. That man destroyed her life, completely, completely. Everything could have been different today," she said sadly.

"Were you close friends?"

"Yes, we appreciated her talent, she painted superbly like a true artist. Then I remember her sitting in the library a lot, he liked to read, and she wrote some poems, which I published in the Sheffield library newsletter. Yes, we were close, she was a sad and lonely soul. No one understood it like I did, absolutely no one," she said eyes closed.

"What do you remember about her death?" Carol asked.

"As I said at the investigation, she was very vulnerable. That bastard made her suffer, his family took her baby too; she had a nervous breakdown. She was not fit to be a mother. She was so fragile..."

"But how did Iris manage to get the pills, where did she get them?"

"I don't know about that, but it wasn't hard to get tablets and she was a clever girl..."

There was a loud knock at the front door, a sign that the residents were coming and had to finish the discussion. Eleonor got up in a hurry and excused herself that they would have to postpone the discussion until later. Gareth said that was enough for now. The girls entered the library, and the room was filled with laughter. Grace and Helen were talking about a movie they had recently seen. Grace saw them and stopped in fright. She looked at Eleonor with a questioning look. She smiled absently and headed towards the computer.

Carol and Gareth had decided to stop for their usual pub lunch on their way to Bradford. It was almost 2:00 pm, but the sky had already darkened.

"I'm inclined to believe that Diane's death is related to her mother's story, but I still don't see why. Iris Clark killed herself because she was abandoned by Brian and because they took her baby. Why did Diane think Iris Clark wouldn't have killed herself, what reason would anyone have to kill her? For all we know, only the Dunmore family would have been interested in her being silenced."

"That's right, but I don't believe that the Dunmore family would have been involved, Diane would have said something."

"What was Diane relying on when she told Steven Morton that she didn't think her mother would kill herself?" Gareth asked.

"Maybe something that someone who was close to Iris would have told him. Eleonor didn't tell us too much. Maybe Deborah? I think that we should check again Iris's investigation file when we get to headquarters," Carol said worriedly. "Then there is something strange about Grace, she is afraid of something, I read in her eyes today."

"Well, all the prisoners are afraid of the police," said Gareth

"No, no, there is something wrong with her," said Carol thoughtfully.

"Do you think Grace could be the murderer? What reason would she have? True, she looks a bit unsettled. We never know about these people…"

"No, our murderer is a cold-blooded person who thought and planned everything in advance. Grace knows something that could give us valuable clues, that's my impression. But she's afraid of someone, maybe she noticed something, but she can't speak."

"I think Eleonor knows something that could give us clues about Diana's death," said Gareth.

"She's a bizarre person, isn't she? But it's not easy to work in this environment for so long, maybe it affects anyone at some point."

“Yes, you can,” said Gareth, looking at his watch. He seemed to have his own concerns about something other than Carol’s assumptions.

“And it seems to be related to the story of Diana’s past. It could be related to the prison management covering up her mother’s death,” Carol said thoughtfully. “I think we need more details about Eleonor’s relationship with Iris, maybe we learn more from Deborah’s statement at the time.”

“I’m sorry Carol, you’ll have to go to the office alone, I must go with my father for a check-up at the eye doctor, we have an appointment at 5.00 pm.”

“It’s not a problem, I’ll read it myself,” answered Carol checking her bill closely.

A Phone Call in the Night

Gareth was about to turn off the lamp for a good and deserved sleep after a heavy dinner and a hectic afternoon in the company of his parents. At the meeting with the oculist, his father had learnt that he needed cataract surgery on his right eye, otherwise he risked losing his sight. He should have done it three years ago when he had surgery on the other eye, but he had stubbornly refused then. Gareth had suggested a second opinion from another doctor, and his suggestion had led to a long discussion about NHS efficiency and professionalism. He had had a difficult relationship with his father all his life. After taking his father home, Gareth decided to remain for dinner at their place, following the insistence of his mother, who wanted more details about the medical visit. As always, the evening spent with his family gave him a feeling of agitation and restlessness. He drank a Belgian beer and mentally reviewed the day.

He turned off the light and threw himself into bed with his arms under his head. On the bedside table, the phone was ringing silently. He thought that maybe he had left something at his parents' house, he could answer tomorrow, there was no rush. A second call came almost immediately. Who would call at this hour so insistently? It was Carol, what happened to her? He decided to take this call.

"Gareth, we need to go to Clayton Prison immediately," Gareth heard Carol on the other end of the phone.

"What is it, what happened?" He asked confused.

"I'll tell you on the way, I'll get to you in 20 minutes, be ready to get off."

"Sure, I will be downstairs," Gareth answered and started to get dressed in a hurry.

Carol arrived in front of his house in 25 minutes.

"What's the rush?" Gareth asked anxiously.

"Grace is in danger, I called the prison to ask them to check her room and they called me back 10 minutes ago, Grace was found unconscious, the ambulance is on the way, I hope she will stay alive. We're going to Clayton now."

"Unconsciousness? Did she try to kill herself?"

"I don't think so," said Carol firmly.

"Do you think someone tried to kill her?"

"More than that, I think I know who tried," said Carol. "We should have realised it earlier. It is Eleanor Wilson. Grace was the weak point in her criminal plan."

"What do you say? What plan?" Gareth asked in astonishment.

"Reading, this evening, the statement given by Deborah in Iris Clark's investigation, I realised. Deborah says there that Iris and Eleonor had an intimate relationship. Iris had told Deborah that Eleanor had become obsessed with her and was very jealous of Brian. As confused as she was, Iris understood Eleonor's true nature. I believe she gave Iris the painkillers and encouraged her to kill herself. Diane thought the same."

"But why would Eleonor do this to Iris if Brian had left? Iris could be with her."

"I think Eleonor wanted revenge. Don't underestimate the passion of a gay couple. Women can be extremely jealous and vindictive. Diane guessed that working with Eleonor, she managed to know her better than anyone. But not enough. She made the mistake of telling Eleanor that she would reveal the truth about Iris in her book. Even if it was an old story, it could create trouble for Eleonor. That's why she made the decision to kill Diane."

"But I saw on the cameras that Eleonor had left the library at the time of Diana's death."

"That's why she needed an accomplice. Grace was perfect. I think Eleonor killed Diane around noon. After Grace left at 11:30, Eleonor went into the Harper Room where Diane was working on processing DVDs. She must have asked her for something from the little storage room. Diane went in there and Eleonor hit her from behind with a heavy object. Unfortunately, police have not yet been able to find the murder weapon. She probably got rid of it after the murder. After making sure Diane was dead, she took off her jacket and belt with her purse and keys, then locked the storage to make sure no one got in there, even if by mistake.

"At 1:00 pm, Grace came into the library, as Eleonor had probably asked her to. Eleonor had a hard say in the committee's evaluations and the residents were aware of it, and so was Grace. Eleonor gave her Diane's jacket and belt with the keys and a blonde wig, prepared in advance. Grace was going to play Diane's role and build Eleonor's alibi. Grace agreed to play it without asking too many questions. As I said, Eleonor is an influential person. Eleonor could help her get a better position and behaviour references. This is why she agreed to help Eleonor. But she is terribly afraid of her."

"You mean Grace had the keys to the prison and went to collect the books?"

"Yes, she played Diane's role perfectly. They were the same height. Besides, at 1 pm, the duty officers changed in all four blocks so that the risk of being recognised by the officers was quite low."

"But it was still."

"It was. Eleonor probably told Grace to avoid talking too much. Grace knows how to act quite well, you've seen. She's not exactly unskilled in the art of disguise, I think she had a bit of fun playing this role. Grace did not know that she had entered a dangerous game with Eleonor. She doesn't have intelligence, unfortunately, she improvised badly, for instance, that sandwich detail was her own idea. It was a big mistake; it caught my attention."

"How about the keys?"

"As we thought, Eleonor wanted to make sure Diane wasn't discovered until the next day. In prison, there is no way to sneak around without being seen. Naturally, there was no way Eleonor could return to the prison unnoticed to set things right as we found them. So that she probably told Grace to leave Diane's jacket and keys in a designated place. She needs to arrange the crime scene. The next morning, she placed the keys and jacket on Diane's body, just as we found them. Unfortunately, that blond hair remained on the jacket. What was the point of Diane wearing a blonde wig?"

"Yes, indeed, it makes sense," Gareth agreed.

"We don't know if Diane took the keys by herself from the officer's cabinet at the entrance or if it was Eleonor who put them on Diane's belt. She had been working in the prison for a long time; she could have her sources to find out the officer's password.

"First, to keep the body hidden until the next morning, when she had time to rearrange the crime scene. Then Eleanor left the keys on Diane's belt to lead us on a false track, specifically to believe that Patterson might be involved. You remember she suggested that from the first day. I believe that Diane occasionally took the officers' keys, probably during Patterson's night shift when she went into the cells and chatted quietly with the girls about whatever she wanted.

"Eleonor's plan had a weak point and *it was Grace*," continued Carol. "Eleonor thought she could manipulate her, but I imagine at a certain point she realised she was wrong. It was probably after hearing about her reaction in the library when I asked Grace about the sandwich story. It was the moment when Eleonor thought of getting rid of Grace. It was only a matter of time before Grace would collapse and throw her out."

"A totally unscrupulous woman. Do you think Deborah died of natural causes?"

"This is hard for me to appreciate. I suppose that it all started with Deborah and her arrival at Clayton. I think Deborah recognised Eleonor after all these years, but she didn't say anything to her. Deborah instead told Diana who was very surprised and started doing a personal investigation. Diane went to Sheffield to talk to Carrie and then studied her mother's death file. Someone in Sheffield must have told Eleanor that Diane was doing research in connection with the investigation into Iris Clark's death. Diane was intelligent and determined to find out the truth about her mother's death.

"I think that by working with Eleonor she managed to know herself better. I think Diane noticed that Eleonor is more attracted to women, especially a certain profile, mentally fragile. The weak and mentally fragile women made Eleonor want to protect them. That is one of the complexities of Eleanor's character. Probably exacerbated by the environment in which she works. Maybe Grace vaguely reminded her of Iris..."

"Yes, indeed, Eleonor seems to have a certain masculinity," said Gareth.

"Agree. I think she truly loved Iris, and her relationship with Brian was quite a shock to Eleonor. She wanted revenge and encouraged Iris' suicidal tendencies. It was a matter of time. Iris was under a lot of pressure after Officer Brian Dunmore's departure. They had taken her little baby. Iris made the decision to put her life at the end. She asked for more antidepressant tablets from Eleonor and she provided them to her lover. In a way, Eleonor was the moral author. Diane knew this and threatened to reveal the truth in her book."

"Then Deborah's arrival at Clayton was terribly bad luck for Eleonor. Otherwise, it would have remained a perfect murder," Gareth said.

"True, Diane stirred up the past. I think in a way, Diane noticed that Eleonor was attracted to Grace Davies. That made her understand that her mother's relationship with Eleonor might be quite credible."

The two detectives had approached Clayton Prison and parked the car in the courtyard next to the ambulance. At the entrance to Block B, the duty officer pointed them to cell number 37 where Grace Davies lived and let them know that a doctor was with her.

Grace was to be taken to the hospital, she was unconscious; the doctor was trying to resuscitate her. Carol and Gareth looked around the room. The cell was in disarray. They noticed two oranges and a chocolate bar on the table. Three unopened envelopes and a mug with coffee in it. Next to the bed, a half-empty Coke bottle and two books.

"Do you think that Grace took sleeping pills?" Carol asked.

"We can't know yet, we must take her to the hospital urgently," answered the doctor.

"We will have to take the coffee cup and the juice bottle for analysis," Carol said and carefully placed them in two sealed plastic bags.

After the ambulance crew left, Gareth went into the duty officer's office to ask for more details about what Grace had done earlier in the evening.

"The officer says he didn't notice anything unusual about Grace Davies tonight," Gareth says. "I checked the girl's schedule for today with him. In the morning, Grace worked in the prison garden with other seven residents, until 11:30 and they had lunch as usual at noon. She stayed on the landing until 5:00 pm when she went to the gym with two other girls. She didn't have dinner, that's quite odd, commented Gareth. She returned to the block at 7:35 pm with the other two girls. Officer Patterson brought them from the gym. There was no incident tonight, they played rummy before bed so until 9:30 when it was time to go out. The officer didn't hear from her again until 10:30 when he got the call from you and went to see if she was okay. Grace didn't answer when he called out to her, so he went in to check on her and then found her unconscious. He called the hospital and asked for an ambulance. Let's hope she escapes."

"It depends on what she took," said Carol. "*Grace is our key witness*. So, you say she didn't work in the library today? Didn't she even see Eleonor today?"

"Apparently not," answered Gareth, examining the notebook as if waiting for its confirmation.

Carol glanced into Grace's cell. She didn't expect to discover anything special. On a small table in front of the window, there were some books on the technique of opening a new business. Next to it, a small TV with a small DVD player and some DVDs. On the wall next to the bed, a few photos of Grace and her daughter, around six years old, Carol assumed. Another photo of Grace riding a horse, smiling widely and happily. In a small wardrobe with three shelves, some clothes, and a pair of stylish sunglasses. The bed was messy. Carol discovers a shoebox under the bed containing a large pile of letters, all from her daughter, Tess. He looked at them, neat and orderly writing.

"I think we have nothing left to find here. She seems to adore her daughter," Carol said after glancing through the letters.

"Yes, we should go now, we'll see how her condition develops tomorrow."

The two detectives thanked the officer on duty who seemed to be busy reporting on the phone about the prisoner's situation. They headed for the car parked in the yard.

The fresh air outside made them feel a bit better. At night, the prison had a scary and sinister look. They didn't talk much on the way back. Carol was driving in silence with her thoughts only, and Gareth was thinking only of the warm bed at home.

Carol Makes Assumptions Again

The mobile phone rang insistently, and Gareth knew it was Carol. He looked at the clock, it was 7:30. He also knew that, more than likely, Carol hadn't slept all night, waiting for news from the hospital about Grace's condition.

"How is Grace?" He asked shortly

"Good news. Grace is out of danger now but can't speak yet."

"Where are you? I'm getting dressed and coming to the office now."

"I'm on my way to the headquarters," said Carol. "Do you want me to pick you up?"

"I didn't dare to ask you this favour, I'm ready right now," said Gareth jumping out of bed.

"I'll arrive in 30 minutes, I'll stop at Costa to get two cups of coffee," said Carol. "I'll offer you a free coffee today."

Gareth knew it had been a long and rough night for Carol. They would probably talk to their boss Mr J this morning about whether they had enough evidence to charge Eleanor Wilson. Carol had probably assessed the situation and checked all night if her theory had any cracks. Grace was their key witness, that was for sure. And Carol had saved her life.

“I’m waiting for the results from the hospital. And the lab tests,” Carol said with a sigh.

“You took them tonight, I suppose?” Gareth said smiling.

“Yes, and I left a message for David, I told him it was urgent.”

“You saved the girl’s life; Mr J will congratulate you.”

“It was intuition, simply. I remember Grace’s scared look yesterday. And after reading Deborah’s statement, it was clear to me the involvement of Eleonor Wilson and the fact that Grace was in danger. However…”

“Is there any doubt? Last night you were fully convinced,” Gareth said.

“Yes, I think we must call Eleonor for an interrogation,” said Carol confidently.

The phone on the desk rang briefly, and Carol immediately picked up the receiver. She listened in silence for a few seconds and his face lit up with a confident expression.

“Grace was poisoned with luminol, a very powerful phenobarbital. And at the laboratory, they found 20 mg in the Coke bottle. She was close to death, it wasn’t a suicide attempt, someone tried to kill her. The murderer wasn’t very careful, it seems and left a little fingerprint on the bottle.”

Eleanor Wilson's Confession

Eleanor Wilson didn't seem surprised when she arrived at the police station for the inquiry. A look of relief appeared on the woman's face hearing that Grace had managed to escape alive.

"What an actress!" Gareth whispered to Carol then invited the woman to sit on a chair in front of the table they were sitting at.

Carol carefully glanced at Eleonor and noticed the deep fatigue on the woman's pale face. The detective noted the apparent self-confidence and detachment. She said in a neutral voice, "You should have told us about this old story with Diane's mother, Iris Clark. It would have saved us a lot of time in the investigation. Do you think you can tell us the truth about what happened then?"

"I didn't think that it could have anything to do with Diane's death. Iris was a special person in my life. After her death, nothing made sense to me. But she lied to me, and I couldn't take it. She was mentally unstable and after they took her child, she became unrecognisable. I couldn't bear to see her collapse."

"Did you get her anti-depressants?"

“ I had to help her, she asked me to help her, I couldn’t let her suffer like this. I didn’t think she would try to kill herself.”

“But you lied to the investigators,” said Gareth.

Eleonor did not answer and kept her gaze on the floor.

“What exactly did Diane tell you about her mother?” Carol asked quietly.

“A few weeks ago, Diane told me she was going to publish a book about her real mother and how she was murdered. I asked her why she was telling me this. She laughed saying she knew I worked at Sheffield Prison 27 years ago when her mother was on life sentence there. She knew about the story with Brian and about my relationship with Iris. Then, Diane said, she knew I couldn’t bear to lose her, so I decided to kill Iris, encouraging her to take painkillers.”

“Then what happened?”

“Diane told me she wanted to reveal this story and revenge her mother’s death. She was saying that the moral blame belonged to me, and not to her father, Brian, who had suffered a life-long trauma.”

“I think it was a big shock for you.”

“Not quite, not exactly. I always knew Diane was Iris’ daughter. I recognised her eyes the first time I saw her. What shocked me was the hatred in her eyes. That was the hardest to bear.”

“That’s why you decided to kill her. You were afraid that the story would be brought back to the attention of the police and the investigation would be reopened.”

“That is ridiculous,” said Eleonor with a confused look, “I didn’t kill Diane. Why would I kill her? There was nothing that could have incriminated me, only a few statements by some prisoners who knew Iris directly or indirectly. My only fault is that I didn't know how to protect Iris, and that has haunted me ever since. No investigation will save me from this and I will live with this guilt for the rest of my life."

The woman seemed to ignore the presence of the two detectives, talking to herself.

Carol stood up and told her she could leave. Gareth looked at his colleague in astonishment and followed her into the office.

"Done, are we done with her?" He asked softly.

"I think she is right. Our criminal is still free. Yet. We must wait for Grace to recover and confirm our theory. As I said, she's our key witness."

The Key Witness Confession

"My intuition was good, then," Gareth said with a victorious twinkle in his eyes.

"Yes, I must admit that it worked well," said Carol smiling.

Grace had recovered a day ago and decided to testify. The fear of death had overcome the fear of telling the truth. She was thinking of her daughter, Tess.

Grace admitted that she had had a relationship with Chris Patterson, who had promised to support her with the application for a reduced sentence. She didn't love him at all, but she had to get out of prison, she missed Tess terribly. How had it all started? A week ago, Chris had approached her in the cell and jokingly asked her if she would like to play Diane's role in a play he was planning. She told him, laughing, that it sounded like fun, and asked him why she would accept the role.

Chris told her he could use his influence to get her a hearing with the commission to reduce her sentence. The dream of seeing Tess again soon seemed more and more achievable. She gladly accepted and he replied that she had to do exactly what he said, without any questions or personal initiative. She had accepted again; she knew that sometimes it was better not to ask questions.

On that Monday, she had arrived at the library in the morning, at 8:45, as usual. She had helped Eleonor with the resident groups. Diane was working in the Harper Room and didn't seem to be on her best days. She seemed in a hurry to finish what she had to do and preoccupied with something else entirely.

Grace finished at 11:30 and headed for her block for her lunch. She returned to the education department with a group of girls who had their math class at 1:40. That's what Chris had asked her to do. The group had been brought by Chris earlier, at 1:30 p.m., when *free movement* began, and he had left them in the math classroom. He had gone to bring another group, for the hairdressing class. Chris had told her that he had planned everything carefully, each minute. Grace was calm and ready for action. The math teacher hadn't arrived yet, so it was easy for her to sneak out of the classroom. Chris had told her to come at 1:45 pm sharp outside the IT room and wait for him to open the door for her. From there, they entered the Harper Room. There was no one there and Chris told her that now she had to play her role.

Chris gave her a blonde wig and a brown jacket, and she assumed it was Diane's jacket. He also gave her Diane's belt and key holder. He explained how to use them, but she already knew. She was going to go to Block C to collect the books from the return box there and bring them back to the library. She had to leave the books behind Eleonor's desk, in the boxes with the other books already collected. Then, Chris had told her she was to hide the wig, jacket, belt, and key holder in a box in the Harper Room. As Chris advised, she had to do this quickly, by 2:10 pm and wait in the library for Kristin's arrival.

The wall clock in the library showed 2:09 when the collection was finished. She still had to tell Kristin that Diane had opened the door for her, that Diane was working in the Harper Room and didn't want to be disturbed. Poor Kristin. How could she be so blind and not see what a scoundrel Chris was? Anyway, the plan had run well. She had barely kept from bursting out laughing as she unlocked the prison gates and saw that no one recognised her. She is such a good actress after all.

Yes, she had lost her temper after realising what had happened to Diane. Good lord! She thought it was an innocent joke. She hadn't imagined it could happen. Then Chris had told her that the police would find Eleanor guilty, who had reason to kill Diane. What could she do? She was in distress and couldn't trust anyone anymore. She had panicked and told Chris Patterson that she would talk to Eleanor and ask her advice. Then it wouldn't have occurred to her that Chris would try to poison her. She had been so naive.

"Poor girl," Gareth had commented. "She didn't know what story he was getting into with this Patterson. He was another victim of this unscrupulous individual."

"I don't know what to say, maybe you're right. But, on the other hand, she agreed to play the play further after the discovery of the body."

Chris Patterson's Confession

The idea to murder Diane had crossed his mind suddenly one evening after she had told him about her research in Sheffield Prison and the involvement of her boss, Eleanor Wilson, in her mother's investigation. A month ago, Diane had told him she wanted a divorce. "Why?" He then asked her. "We get along very well that way, with our separate lives," he had told her. "Kristin is not important to me, you know that. Did you meet someone?" He had asked Diane.

"It's none of your business, but I'm tired of sponsoring you," Diane had replied cynically.

Then he remembered why he hated Diane. She had always managed to surprise him. Just when he thought he knew her better, Diane would make a move that left him speechless. At first, he had resigned himself to the idea that he would be able to get an amount of money in the divorce that would ensure his comfort for a while. Then, one evening, after she had told him about her research, an interesting scenario had taken shape in his mind. He couldn't count on or involve Kristin, and she was suspicious and fearful anyway. Eleanor Wilson's old story and Diane's desire for revenge could be good context, he had thought then that Eleanor could be the perfect murderer.

The opportunity had come when Kristin had told her that Eleonor was having problems with her daughter. Eleonor Wilson used to leave some afternoons to go to therapy with her daughter. The plan could only be started in her absence from the library. Eleanor Wilson would let her colleagues know when she had to leave so he had time to prepare a plan of action. The alibi had to be prepared carefully. Grace could play Diane's role, they were the same height, with little make-up, wig, and matching clothes, no one would have guessed it wasn't Diane. It was simple to convince Grace and easy to keep her under control. At least that's what he thought at first. Then he swapped with Rob, his colleague, to do the Monday night shift.

Last Monday seemed like the perfect day to act. He had told Diane that Grace had decided to talk about her relationship with Eleanor. Diane was going to talk to Grace in her cell after dinner, quietly. He arranged with Diane to meet in the library at 1:40 pm to have lunch together and discuss the details. He had brought a group of prisoners, including Grace, to math class, then entered the library through the IT room, where he knew there was no CCTV camera. Diane was waiting for him, anxious to hear the details about meeting Grace that evening. Diane had already taken the keys for the officers, using his passcode. She had asked him how he had managed to persuade Grace to talk. When she'd entered the storage, it hadn't been hard for him to hit her on the head with a stapler a few times. He had it ready in his pocket. Short and to the point. Diane died almost immediately.

He removed her jacket and the belt with the set of keys and quickly locked the storage door. He also took her car key. He had to get rid of Diane's laptop and phone, just in case. As he thought, they were in the car, and he was going to hide them in the garage. At 1:45, Grace arrived, as they had arranged, in front of the IT room. She played Diane's role perfectly. His alibi was secured. He left the library to take the other group of residents to the hairdresser class. He only came back after midnight, also through the IT room, to check and prepare for the crime scene.

He dressed Diane in her jacket and put on the belt, and purse with keys. He made sure he didn't leave any clues. He had already taken the stapler and thrown it in a trash can on his way to town. He also put the car key in Diane's pocket. Everything seemed to be going smoothly until Grace threatened to speak to Eleanor Wilson. This he hadn't foreseen, and he understood that he had to eliminate her quickly.

It wasn't difficult to get Luminal tablets and slip them into the Coke bottle that he gave to Grace on their way back from the gym. He knew she liked Coke. The quick intervention of the detectives messed up his plans. He didn't have time to get the fingerprints off the Coke bottle.

"How did he manage to get into the *Harper Room* from the IT room?" Gareth had asked.

"I asked myself too. Apparently, he had duplicated the key from Eleonor Wilson's drawer a long time ago. Diane had helped him, ironically. Patterson occasionally arranged various nocturnal meetings with female prisoners in the *Harper Room*. He knew that the entrance was not monitored with camera CCTV. Eleanor Wilson had no idea about Patterson's meetings with female prisoners late at night in the Harper Room. Neither did Diane."

"As I said, an unscrupulous chap," said Gareth.

“He tried from the beginning to manipulate us with this story about Eleonor Wilson’s past. But, as we know, no plan can be perfect.”

Epilogue

They had found Diane's laptop hidden in a small closet in the garage. Patterson had been right. Diane was working on a novel about her mother's life.

"Patterson didn't destroy the laptop because he intended to bring it to us and thus incriminate Eleonor Wilson," said Carol. "*The Sad Story of the Wild Iris* is really the story of the sad fate of her mother, Iris Clarck."

"Do you think it is inspired by reality?" Gareth asked.

"That's what I say. I think Deborah gave Diane information about Iris Clark. Deborah was her mother's friend and knew more about Iris's life than anyone. Diane would have been a good writer. I disagree with your colleague who said Diane had no writing talent. She also added imagination and fantasy inspired by his mother's paintings."

"It's a shame that she didn't manage to publish it," said Gareth. "Her family will not agree to this novel being published."

" I agree with you. Too bad, really. We worked well together on this case, do you agree, Gareth?" Carol said smiling.

"Sure, as always. I would even say that we could have closed the case faster if we had followed my precious instinct."

Carol laughed and suggested going out for a rewarding lunch before they started working on the final report of the investigation.